When It All Falls Apart

Lawrence Etienne

ISBN 978-1-64299-258-8 (paperback)
ISBN 978-1-64299-259-5 (digital)

Christian Faith Publishing, Inc.
832 Park Avenue
Meadville, PA 16335
www.christianfaithpublishing.com

Printed in the United States of America

Dedication

First and foremost, I want to thank God for bringing out the gift within me to write this book. Together, we did it Lord! It is also dedicated to my parents and wife for their incredible love and support. Finally, I want to acknowledge my two sons for their continued encouragement throughout the writing of this novel. You guys are the greatest and being your dad is truly a blessing!

Contents

Chapter 1

... In the Beginning

———◆———

"Why in the hell did you do this to me? All I ever tried to do was make you and our children happy!" Before an answer was muttered, thoughts of a happier time consumed the both of them.

Jasmine Carver was a well-educated woman from a modest family that settled in Ball Ground, Georgia. She received an engineering degree from Georgia Southern University in 1995. Two years prior to etching her name in stone as her family's first college graduate, she met Michael Fletcher on campus during a scheduled study hall for the basketball players. She often looked for ways to supplement her income; therefore, when the opportunity was presented, she began to earn extra money working as a tutor for the athletic department. Instantly, Michael caught her eye, as he seemed to glide into the library where the sessions were being held. He stood six feet, six inches and tipping the scale at a solid two hundred and twenty-five pounds. The junior college transfer and native Houstonian was the talk of the campus months before his arrival, as basketball enthusiasts memorized his accomplishments on the hardwood as if they were taking a world history exam. Michael was a polite gentleman and appeared to have his priorities in order. Those who knew him would utter harmonious sentiments concerning his character and religious beliefs. As Jasmine waited patiently for the next available student-athlete to park their egotistical, pompous, overbearing, privileged posterior in the empty seat in her tutoring cubbyhole, she found it difficult to remain calm as she secretly wanted Michael to fill the available seat next to her. She drifted for only a moment as she pictured him as the man from her most romantic dream. As she hoped, Michael appeared and answered her prayers. Shortly after their first encounter, Jasmine went to Ball Ground for a weekend getaway. While family and friends gathered at her parents' home, Jasmine revealed her innermost lovey-dovey feelings for Michael. She felt that day in the study hall was a divine confirmation from God that her husband had arrived! Although the NBA didn't send the paparazzi to welcome Michael as a professional basketball player, he completed his goal by graduating with a degree in music from Georgia Southern as well. Time passed and their adoration for each other grew stronger with every rising of the sun. As it became obvious, marriage was the next phase for their lives. Michael tossed and turned each night for months, desperately searching for a creative way to pop the big question to the woman worthy of his love. After scanning his brain for countless hours, he finally devised the perfect plan. Prior to moving to Texas to join her version of Denzel, Jasmine found gainful employment working for a very renowned engineering firm in Houston. They didn't believe in shacking up. Therefore, Michael stayed with his parents while Jasmine moved into her apartment. He knew it was temporary as the plan was to purchase a home after they got married.

Her transition was easy. She settled into her career and experienced opportunity sooner than anyone expected. Although she was the least experienced engineer in the firm, her superiors felt she was perfect to head a very lucrative project with Hunter's Architectural Innovations. The two companies were planning to unite in hopes of ushering in the most revolutionary high-rise condominiums in Houston's flourishing downtown. A very important meeting was scheduled to finalize the plans in the conference room of Hunter's Architectural Innovations. About a month later, Jasmine and her superiors arrived on schedule, as they confidently exited the company's limousine. Pedestrians walking by seemed to pause in reverence to royalty walking down the legendary red carpet into the corporate building. Her eyes mirrored the confidence of Steve Jobs introducing a new Apple product while simultaneously ignoring the butterflies that moved inside of her stomach like dancers moving to the beat of a hot techno song. Nevertheless, she walked elegantly, stride for stride with Mr. Stevenson and sons. James Stevenson was the founder and CEO of Jasmine's firm and was a very wise man. His colleagues admired him for leading people with a heart of gold. Some employees even categorized him as the wise grandfather that is always available to share wisdom. Mr. Stevenson was eight days short of seventy-one years old. He was a small man in stature, yet a very powerful pillar in the business arena. Mr. Stevenson was happily married for forty-eight years to Elisa Stevenson, until her battle with breast cancer claimed her life at the age of sixty-nine. They raised three boys on a farm in St. Martinsville, Louisiana, all while Mr. Stevenson completed his undergraduate course work at a nearby university. Their oldest son graduated from LSU with a pharmacy degree. The younger boys followed the footsteps of their father, receiving engineering degrees from the University of Houston. As board members in their father's firm, they were instrumental in recruiting and acquiring the talents of Jasmine Carver. Several skeptics within the firm began many of their days at the coffee pot and water cooler giving their opinion on how she was chosen to head the project. Everyone came to the consensus that Mr. Stevenson chose her because she was a second coming of his late dear wife. Even the skeptics were astonished by Jasmine's striking resemblance of the photo Mr. Stevenson had in a very expensive, mahogany frame hanging on the wall directly facing his desk. The photo memorialized the essence and beauty of a young, vibrant

Mrs. Elisa Stevenson. If you were in his office when the sun illuminated the room, you would instantly notice an inexplicable halo that appeared above Mrs. Stevenson's head. This mystifying act of God brought refuge to Mr. Stevenson's spirit because he believed, without a shadow of a doubt, this was God's way of allowing him to peek into heaven and see his wife as she rested in God's glory.

The power group from Stevenson Engineering entered the building with their game face on. Every step Ms. Carver took provided necessary portions of boldness and poise to seal the deal for the firm. As they reached the elevator, Mr. James, as they often referred to Stevenson, whispered to Jasmine in a motivating tone, "God has prepared you for this moment. Let him speak through your spirit and you will discover he is the master at sealing deals." After encouraging Jasmine, he gave her a wink and smile. She smiled back and took note of how suave and charismatic the old man could be. After receiving the final locker room speech, she seemed to lace up and take the field like a Hall of Fame quarterback destined for glory. Soon after, they walked into the conference room. In the back of the room was a burgundy, hand-stitched, silk tablecloth adorned with Japanese artwork draping over a long table. On top of the table, Jasmine noticed wine glasses and what seemed to be expensive bottles of vintage wine arranged perfectly on the left end. Fruit and vegetable trays, cocktail shrimp, and an array of sauces revolved around an impeccable flower arrangement to complete the masterpiece.

Surely, this was prepared for the celebration that was to come. Suddenly, the architectural team walked in with a serious, yet cordial demeanor. Craig Knowles headed up the project on their side and like a ringside bell in a heavyweight fight, confident handshakes and greetings were extended to set things in motion and the game was on! Percentages, projections, surveys, tax breaks, profit, and cost were being thrown around like a major cafeteria food fight. Impressively, Ms. Carver seemed to thrive in that environment. She boldly explained how Stevenson Engineering was the perfect partner for their firm. She spoke so eloquently. The room silenced as if they wanted more of the gifted speaker. When the dust settled, smiles and handshakes were passed around as if a newborn baby was introduced to the world. After speaking at a rate of speed and precision that caused a severe case of cottonmouth, Jasmine was ready for a nice glass of wine. However, before she could encompass her mind with that thought, Mr. Knowles cleared his throat and said, "Ladies and gentlemen, if I could have your attention, I realize this is a great day for both firms; however, there is one more item on the agenda that we must address or should I say, Ms. Carver needs to address to complete our business here today. Wilson will you please?"

Like a confused schoolgirl, the Georgian whipped her head around to look at Mr. James and sons and whispered, "What in the world is he talking about?" They simply replied with their hands in the air and shrugging their shoulders in unison like three confused synchronized swimmers. Her hands began to drip with sweat, as anxiety began to set in. Before she could emit another word, Wilson turned off the lights. She took a deep breath as the projection screen began to descend. Everyone sitting in the room examined her expressions with intrigued faces. Undoubtedly, this added to her panicked condition. The projector began to play and panic turned into complete shock as she stared at the screen in bewilderment. She leaned forward and said to Mr. Knowles, "Where did you get my baby pictures? OK, what's going on?" Craig gave the same reply Mr. James had given minutes prior. The slide show displayed a collection of pictures from her days at Georgia Southern. Many of them were pictures of her courtship with Michael as soft music played throughout the surround sound in the room. Once the slide show was over, the lights were turned on and Michael stood next to the adorned table in the back of the room with a bouquet of red roses and a black velvet box in his hands. Jasmine was absolutely speechless. He walked toward Jasmine and began to kneel before her. Although the slide show was over, the soft music played on. Like a scene from a movie, Michael began, "I was raised to trust God with my life, believing he wants what's best for me. I learned at an early age to seek a loving relationship with him, and by doing so, he would reward my love for him with an angel. I truly feel you are God sent. You are my gift from heaven and I vow to be a man of integrity and take care of the gift God has bestowed on me. Jasmine, with every fiber of my being, I will cling to you as my wife, my friend, and my blessing. Ms. Carver, will you bless my life by taking my hand in marriage?" As Michael concluded, every woman in the room had tears rolling down their cheeks. Nearly hyperventilating, Jasmine was only able to cover her mouth with trembling hands, and blurred vision from the pool of tears in her eyes, while answering her prince with an animated nod of acceptance. "Now, the deal is official!" Mr. James shouted. The room instantly filled with laughter.

Michael was a very thoughtful man. He seemed to thrive in situations that challenged his creativity. His originality was a product of his gift for music. He had dreams to not only produce music for major artists but also produce original soundtracks for the film industry. After graduating, he had early success working with local gospel and jazz artists in Houston. However, he knew in order to establish himself as an up and coming music producer, working out of town for months upon end or relocating to a major market was a probable scenario.

Once they were married, their life was taking shape. However, Michael had to make a tough decision early on. He passed on a legitimate opportunity to move to a musical-landmarked city when a country band based in Nashville requested his expertise. They wanted him to be the lead producer for their album. The only problem Michael faced was relocating to Nashville to work closely with the band. The timing could not have been any worse. His life with

Jasmine was perfect. She had agreed to uproot from her Georgia roots and follow him to Texas, and in addition, landed her dream job. He didn't want her to feel she was the reason he didn't make it, in case this was his first and last chance to break into the industry. Therefore, when he received the phone call, he contemplated not telling her about the opportunity. Jasmine knew he had something on his mind, but she also knew he would not be forthcoming with the CIA -leveled intelligence he acquired during his phone call. She waited to give him time to debrief, as she placed the dirty clothes into the washing machine. After doing so, she walked into the bedroom where Michael sat in a chair next to their bay window with his head resting in his hands, slipping into deep thought. For many guys, the decision to take advantage of this opportunity would be a no brainer, but Michael was somewhat different. He understood the sacrifices Jasmine made to prove she trusted his judgment for their lives. He felt it would be extremely selfish to only think of what he wanted. Jasmine began, "So anything you would like to talk about?" Lifting his head, Michael gave her a look that suggested he wasn't in the mood to verbalize what he was feeling. However, Jasmine was poised to break his line of defense and find out what was causing his apparent state of depression. She continued, "I know something is bothering you and I think it's unfair for you to shut me out. We are supposed to be a team. How can I help you if you don't include me when things are on your mind?"

Understanding Jasmine's point of view, Michael decided there wasn't going to be a better time to discuss his dilemma. He reluctantly began, "Well, that was the manager of the Crawford Boys, a country band from Nashville, and they want me to come aboard as a lead producer on their next project."

Jasmine had an astounded look on her face and responded, "Well, Fletch, as she often called him, what is the reason for the long face? I would imagine you being excited about this opportunity."

Michael stood up and walked toward Jasmine as she stood in the doorway of their bedroom. He grabbed her hands, gently pulled her close to him, and softly exclaimed, "I am very excited about the chance to break into the industry; however, it would require me to relocate and move to Nashville. I'm torn because it would mean either I ask you to walk away from your job or we agree to be together and live apart. Unfortunately, I won't be happy with either decision. So I can't accept the project."

Jasmine listened and couldn't help feeling she was the obstacle in his way. She encouraged Michael to follow his dreams, as she reassured him things would work out. Michael, being a spiritual man, simply replied, "I feel God will send another opportunity that will be best for you and me. I am going to turn down this project and have faith that something better will come along. In the meantime, I think I will look for a building to open a studio and build my clientele. Maybe, eventually, I'll get clients like the Crawford Boys to come to Houston to work."

Jasmine seemed to float on his every word, understanding she was in love with a man with vision. At that moment, her heart fluttered with admiration for a man who purposely put her first. She knew she was blessed to have him in her life.

Years later, Michael and Jasmine's storybook marriage produced two handsome boys. Brandon Fletcher was the oldest child. He was a very intelligent young man, and from an early age, it was easy to predict he would be very athletic. Chris was twenty months younger than Brandon, but equally mature. As a toddler, he seemed to be very inquisitive. He didn't mind asking questions to get a clear understanding about things that intrigued him. The boys both were very considerate kids with huge hearts. Their compassion would always lead them to try and give money to the homeless and those less fortunate that stood helplessly at intersections throughout the city. Many times when Michael would come to a stop at a red light, he would purposely turn and watch whoever is occupying the front passenger seat. On cue, the occupant would scramble through the ashtray where he kept his loose change in search for quarters, dimes, and nickels for those in need. The chill he felt from seeing his boys have a heart for humanity never got old. Considering many kids their age only cared about themselves, Michael and Jasmine were blessed to have compassionate children. Brandon was embarking on his freshman year in high school, while Chris was preparing to stroll the seventh grade hallways. The Fletchers were a close-knit family and often joked around. The kitchen was a commonplace for family time and occasional comedy hour. One Saturday morning while having breakfast, Mrs. Fletcher expressed her excitement about going to Georgia for a vacation. Brandon instantly responded, "Come on, Mom! Don't depress me while I'm trying to enjoy my cereal."

Jasmine's crew would occasionally joke about the lack of entertainment in Ball Ground each year there is talk of a dreaded Carver family reunion. She would always respond by placing her left hand on her hip and say, "I may be a small town girl, but that small town groomed me to be a major player in the big city!" She would always remind them that Ball Ground was once featured on a national news segment as one of America's holy towns. Reporters interviewed citizens of the small community of 1,400 Georgians for a piece that focused on the benefits of the entire community closing businesses to worship together on Sunday mornings. Chris and Brandon had a look they would give each other when they felt their parents said something corny. Immediately after Jasmine finished, Chris looked at Brandon and then turned to Jasmine and said, "Mom, you're lame!" The boys laughed with brotherly love and headed outside to begin their yard work. Meanwhile, Michael laughed as he turned his back to pour a cup of coffee. Jasmine and Michael felt it was important to talk to their children about how they view the world. Michael was known as "Rev." around the house because he would have heart to heart talks with the boys about life and more importantly what God required of them. While adding an excessive amount of sugar to his coffee, he solicited Jasmine's feelings on an upcoming topic for the boys. Michael began to speak with a concerned look on his face, "Well, the boys are growing up and I'm afraid it's time for THE TALK! I've been dreading this, but I believe it's time to sit them down and see where they are on the matter."

Jasmine leaned back in her seat, crossed her legs, softly blew the steam from her coffee, and said, "Why are you stressing? Don't worry yourself to death over it. Just give them some condoms and tell them you're not giving them the green light to have sex. However, if they decide to go that route, by all means be safe." Jasmine's advice didn't go over well with Michael. He felt his wife was a little passive on the matter.

Chapter 2

...A Difference in Opinions

Like any other marriage, the Fletchers had their share of disagreements. Many times, arguments ended with both sides agreeing to disagree. However, Michael felt this issue required a united front. What had started as a morning chat over a cup of coffee began to take form of a slugfest between two shade tree lawyers determined to win their case. While leaning against the wall next to the refrigerator, Michael folded his arms and began to explain, "I'm going to assume you were joking, because if you're not, we have a lot to talk about. First of all, I want them to understand what is required of them by God, regardless of what the world considers acceptable. There's no way I'm going to indirectly give the boys my consent to occasionally fall off the horse and disobey God's word. Don't get me wrong; I'm not being naive thinking they will never deviate from what they've been taught. I just feel as their parents, we should take the biblical approach."

As Michael concluded, Jasmine nodded as she raised her eyebrows to indicate she understood his view, yet she had a rebuttal. "I have always agreed with raising our kids according to biblical principles; however, I would feel better if they knew what precautions to take if they made the decision to have sex. I know you have your own philosophy on how the boys should live, but I feel you are not leaving room for error. The last thing we will want is the boys to abandon their spiritual values altogether and follow their fleshly desires because being the perfect Christian is too hard of a job."

The conversation went on for another thirty minutes, before taking a break from deliberations. Over the years, Jasmine matured into taking a more practical approach to things. Many would say her views were more mainstreamed, as opposed to her husband's beliefs. Michael's apprehensiveness to talk to the boys was a mere icebreaker before discussing a more touchy issue that still went unresolved. Later that evening, talks resumed. The Fletchers were at war over Jasmine's brother and his fiancée moving into their home, in efforts of establishing a life in Houston. Jason Carver still lived in Georgia and refused to be a mainstay in the Ball Ground community. Jasmine didn't have a problem with it at all, while Michael felt it wasn't wise to let an unwedded couple shack up in their house. He was old fashioned in his thinking and living together was only a den for daily sin. He was adamant that type of behavior would not take place in his home. Jasmine was furious with his decision! She felt he was out of line to assume her brother would purposely disrespect their home. At the end of the day, it was her brother and she wasn't going to turn him away. Jasmine rarely fought with Michael once he presented adequate reasons why the family should do certain things. However, she felt he would not have been so absolute if it was his family asking to stay. He told Jasmine it didn't matter whose family member it was, he still would feel the same way. Jasmine was so angry; she had an impulse to throw a glass against the wall. Many times, she felt Michael was a hypocrite. There were several instances when his actions contradicted his beliefs. Yet he often continued to take a self-righteous stance as if his judgment was as fair as Lady Justice. Oftentimes, the boys would tease him and ask, "Dad, before you make a ruling, shouldn't you put on your blindfold and hold a scale in your hand?" If it was one thing that irritated her about Michael, it was his inability to compromise. He seemed to be disconnected when it came to issues that were important to her. Jasmine contemplated bringing up a terrible incident that took place a year ago, when he agreed to help his younger sister and cosign for her condo. He knew she had an older boyfriend that only used her when he wanted something.

Jasmine tried to tell Michael, "Eventually, she's going to allow that dead beat to come and take over her apartment." Although Jasmine had valid reasons for saying that, her opinion was overlooked. Often, Michael's sister, Alexis, would call Jasmine crying because her low-life boyfriend was either seen riding around in her car with other women, or he would receive late night phone calls that led him away from the bedroom. Alexis begged her not to tell Michael about her relationship problems; however, Jasmine felt obligated to tell him what his sister was going through. The last thing she wanted was to sit on a secret and something happened. In a loving way, she explained to Alexis the position she was in. Although Alexis preferred she didn't tell her big brother, she understood her sister-in-law was caught in the middle. When Jasmine sat him down and informed him, Michael was furious and vowed to have a long talk with his sister. Jasmine suggested he call her and discuss it over the phone.

"I'm not going to discuss this over the phone. I'm fed up with Alexis and the piss poor decisions she's making with her life!"

However, he did call to see if she was home. When Alexis didn't stay with her parents, she would secretly stay with Ray Burkes, her good-for-nothing boyfriend. He never had a stable home. He merely persuaded the younger Alexis to freeload with him. They simply migrated from house to house of his family and friends until wearing out their welcome. Alexis didn't answer, so he called his mom to see if she knew of her whereabouts. As fate would have it, his sister was there. Once his mother told him what he needed to know, he headed to his parents' house. Michael anxiously walked into his mom and dad's home prepared to demand that his sister leaves Ray alone! Upon entrance, he saw

Alexis sitting in the dining room snacking on a bowl of grapes. Her nonverbals suggested she was all set for their conversation. His parents sat in the family room waiting for the reinforcements, as if Michael was the FBI's head negotiator stepping into the command trailer on the scene of a hostile situation. They also felt it was a wise choice for Michael to talk to his sister. Alexis's relationship with Burkes was affecting her bond with her parents. Despite her terrible decision to date the opposite of her father and big brother, Alexis was a delightful young lady. As a little girl, she hung on every word her father would speak. He would do all the fatherly things with her that you would see in the movies that normally warmed the hearts of the audience. It was common for the two of them to take trips to the ice-cream shop, adventures to the zoo, and picnics in the park and stand united as coach and athlete at her gymnastics competitions.

Unfortunately, Mr. Fletcher felt the memories that he cherished were becoming distant in his daughter's mind. His suspicions were valid, as Alexis had begun to turn a deaf ear to his attempts to convince her to leave Ray Burkes. After quickly taking notice of the calm atmosphere that surrounded a stressful situation, Michael adjusted his approach. He walked into the family room and greeted his parents in a normal tone as he does on every visit. Before he could turn and place his focus on Alexis, his mother stood near the fireplace and made a hand gesture to call him over to give him some pointers before he lectured Alexis.

"Michael, before you go in to talk to your sister, remember she is defensive; and if you start with a demanding tone, she will just tune you out. Understand she is confused and believes she is in love. You don't want to start by attacking Ray. Try getting her to focus on the positive male figures in her life. I think that would give you a better chance of getting her to understand what is at stake."

Michael agreed, "All right, Mom, you may be right."

Once again, as he turned toward the dining room, his father whispered, "Son, do not let her manipulate you with her spoiled innocent routine."

Michael couldn't resist smiling as he responded, "Oh, you mean don't fall for the daddy's little girl routine she uses on you? Don't worry, I'm not that gullible."

Michael's mother moved from the fireplace to the sit on the sofa. She crossed her legs and shook her head saying, "Lord, this is about to be interesting."

With the confidence of a solider, Michael walked into the dining room and took a seat at the dinner table directly across from Alexis. Ziggie, the family's beloved Shih Tzu walked over and placed his front paws on Alexis's chair indicating he wanted to sit in her lap. Ziggie knew when Alexis was happy and he sensed when she was sad and needed to rub him like a breathing stress ball. He loved to be at her side whenever she entered the room. Like a mother and child, Alexis gently rubbed his head and said, "Ziggie, go get in your bed. I'll be OK."

Amazingly, he tilted his head to the right and exposed his big beautiful eyes as to say, "Are you sure?"

Alexis responded while applying one last stroke of assurance across his well-groomed coat, "Go on, I'll be fine."

On cue, Ziggie scampered out of the dining area and headed upstairs to his doggie bed. Before speaking, Michael looked into Alexis's eyes as if he was establishing dominance. Subsequently, Alexis returned the stare. However, shortly thereafter, she lowered her head rendering herself as the subordinate. It was like a scene between a male and female lion.

"First and foremost Alexis, I am here because I love you dearly. I didn't come to judge you. However, I do have my opinion of your lifestyle and this guy you are involved with. Jasmine did tell me some things you guys talked about and I'm hurt."

Alexis interrupted, "Hurt, why are you hurt, Michael? The things I've gone through with Ray don't have anything to do with you. I know you are concerned, but ya'll need to let me live my life. I know what I'm doing."

As Michael allowed Alexis the floor, he heard the innocence in her voice. "I'm hurt because it seems you have completely ignored the examples you have in Dad and me. We are examples of the type of man you should want. From birth, you've been treated like a princess. Dad spent more time with you and gymnastics than he ever did with me playing ball.

You never hear him cursing Mom out and calling her names. He treats her like a lady. I hear this dude Ray calls you everything except the child of God. He cheats on you, takes your car for days at a time, and doesn't work. Why are you with him?"

Alexis began to get agitated as she listened to Michael. She stood up and began to walk near the window. "Michael, I love him. Yes, he has done things to hurt me, but he has done some good things too."

Michael instantly fired back, "Oh yeah, like what?"

Alexis knew she didn't have enough examples to build Burkes up, so she began to fold. "I know I deserve better than Ray, but sometimes, I feel he just needs a little more time to get on track."

Michael added, "Sounds like you have been brainwashed into seeing the small amount of good in him and using that as your reason to stay with him."

Alexis sluggishly nodded in agreement, "I know God has better for me, but what if my job is to change him?"

Michael couldn't hold back the urge to respond abruptly, "Change him? Are you mentally ill? God has never given anyone the assignment of changing people! And that's because you can't change people! Even God himself gives us the free will to choose. If you want better, you gotta fight to have better. You've settled for a man that tells you everything you want to hear. If you spend time telling this dude everything you are lacking in your life, he will make note of it and pretend to have your best interest at heart.

He will try to make very minor efforts look like big sacrifices. This man is using you for sex and what money you can bring to the table! You need a plan to break all ties with him. I'm talking physically, mentally, and emotionally."

Alexis began to form tears in her eyes as she timidly mumbled, "What about spiritually?"

Understanding his sister was blinded by what she thought was love; he softly placed his left hand on her shoulder and gently wiped the tears from her eyes with his right finger. He looked deep into her eyes with brotherly love and whispered, "Lexi, that's just it. You are not spiritually tied to him. You have allowed yourself to be drawn physically to this guy and the emotions may be so strong, to where you feel you connect with his inner man. What this man is doing to you isn't promoting your spirit. He is a distraction from what God has for you. Never look to spiritually connect with a person that has no spiritual connection with God."

As their parents eavesdropped, they looked at each other and spoke simultaneously, "Michael is good!"

Michael felt things went well, so he decided to end the conversation on a good note. "So I hear you got that promotion you were praying for."

Alexis smiled and instantly filled with excitement, "Yeah it came down to me and a lady from Boston. I couldn't believe I was chosen considering she had more experience. I told Mom if I got the promotion, I would start looking for my own place."

Michael nodded in approval, "So have you started looking? If you need anything, just let me know."

"Really? Well it just so happens I'm thinking about getting a condo in the downtown area. It's very upscale. I started the paperwork and I may need a cosigner."

"Well, you can count on me."

Michael trusted Alexis would rid herself of Ray Burkes and restart her quest for love. When he returned home, Jasmine was sitting in the family room waiting to debrief the evening's proceedings.

"So how did it go?" Michael placed his cell phone and keys on the bar and sat next to his wife.

"Believe it or not, it went well. I mean it was like she wanted to hear someone confirm what she already felt inside. I think she really wants better than this Burkes character. Oh yeah, she found a condo downtown and asked me to cosign for her."

Jasmine chose her words carefully before inquiring about the real estate deal Michael verbally committed too. "Before you sign anything, are you sure Alexis understands her boyfriend isn't allowed to take over?"

"Come on, Jasmine, after tonight, she knows what I expect. I didn't have to bring that up."

Jasmine shook her head in disgust. "OK, if things turn out differently, don't go on a rampage."

Three months passed, and Alexis moved into her luxurious condo. She was single, empowered, and content with being alone until the right guy came along. Although being without Ray Burkes was difficult to cope with at times, she was determined to move beyond his emotional grip that lingered in her heart. In search of a little relaxation, Alexis walked out her building to meet some girlfriends. As she waited for her car to arrive from valet, she noticed a man across the street that resembled Ray Burkes. It was like he was inserted into Alexis's day like an extra in a movie. When she processed everything, she knew it was indeed, Ray Burkes! Alexis thought, "What is he doing here? Lord, I don't want to deal with this today." Her heart was beating faster and her hands began to sweat. She couldn't believe how quickly her heart reverted back to the emotional attachment she had for Ray. It seemed she forgot about her conviction to walk all the way with God. Ray brought out a certain erotic side of her. She felt the need to impress him when he was present. He made eye contact with her and gave an arrogant smile. His nonverbal expressions suggested he was in total control of her heart. As he crossed the street to join her, Alexis faintly called on God for strength to withstand Ray's advances. However, deep down inside, she really didn't want to resist his advances.

"Hi, beautiful lady! Don't be nervous. I only wanted to see you and say a few things to you. I know you are trying to move on with your life, and by no means am I trying to get in your way. Shannon told me you were doing well. I kind of talked her into telling me where you lived. So please don't be upset with her. I just wanted you to know that I love you from the bottom of my heart. Seeing you move on caused me to look at myself and want better for both you and me. I guess I came today because I want you to understand I'm willing to change in order to have you in my life."

Ray always had a luring tongue. His sincere delivery always seemed to captivate Alexis. He knew she had a soft heart. He also knew she would struggle turning him away. Alexis listened without an expression on her face. Ray's trance didn't appear to affect her. However, an inner skirmish was taking place. Better yet, a raging battle was in full effect between her flesh and spirit. Her flesh wanted to cancel all her plans and take him up to her condo and let him have his way with her. It was a classic case of David vs. Goliath. Her spirit searched the biblical grounds of her soul for a rock and slingshot to slay Ray's grip. As the spirit scrambled for ammunition, the flesh spoke to her like the sneaky friend convincing her to do whatever, whenever, and wherever.

"You are grown and sexy, girl! This man wants to change for you. This is what you've been waiting for. Take him upstairs and show him how much you've missed him. This is a sign the two of you were meant for each other!"

Instantly, she envisioned Ray's hands passionately caressing her body. She desperately wanted to justify her lust for Ray; therefore, she convinced her spirit to consider this encounter as God working in mysterious ways. Needless to say, Alexis never made it to the day spa. Eventually, Ray was given a key to the condo. Alexis basically forced herself to see a change in Burkes. Unfortunately, he never changed. Ray was the same manipulative man that swindled his way through just about everything. He used Alexis in the past and appeared to pick up where he left off. Every week, he added things to an empty drawer in Alexis's dresser. It went from a couple of T-shirts and socks in the drawer to shoes in the closet, slacks, and button-down shirts hanging on his side of the rack. He began sleeping there at least four times a week. To make it look good, he would occasionally buy groceries and pick up around the house. However, he remained unemployed and showed no signs of pursing an honest day's pay. Yet Alexis felt he just needed time to land a job he really wanted. When Michael and Jasmine would ask to come by after church, she would either make excuses to keep them away or she would make sure Ray and his belongings were out of sight. Before long, the condo took on Ray's taste and Alexis was more like the visitor. He began having his undesirable friends over to watch the game, play cards, and discuss ways to make money. Before reuniting with Alexis, Ray and his friends were often involved in robberies, drug deals, using and selling stolen credit cards, as well as passing counterfeit money. Their crime ring became very organized. As business began to expand, Ray would bring drugs and stolen credit cards to the condo and hide them while Alexis was working. Burkes and his crew quickly graduated to dealing major shipments of cocaine and crystal meth. The credit card scam became recreational. Meanwhile, they used the counterfeit money to buy the drugs from their supplier. Needless to say, scamming their supplier with counterfeit money was reason enough to sleep with both eyes open. Alexis seemed oblivious to Ray's movements. All she focused on was legitimizing her revamped relationship, in order to convince her family Ray was a changed man.

Soon after the drug business appeared to be flowing smoothly, Ray began to shower Alexis with jewelry and clothes. He knew eventually she would ask where the money was coming from. In order to explain the sudden rise in income, Ray told Alexis he found a job working offshore. That eliminated explaining late night arrivals or simply not coming home for days at a time. Ray went as far as to have fake pay stubs printed to show Alexis upon her request to support his charades. Burkes and his crew began to take over a section of the city, as they dealt directly with drug cartels from South America. However, he rolled the dice one too many times with the counterfeit money. Since Burkes had established a business relationship with the Mexican cartel, he simply sent the money and they shipped the product without the dramatic exchange in an abandon warehouse you might see in the movies. Ray had several suppliers. Many of them he swindled with counterfeit money. However, he never took chances with the Mexicans. He knew it would be war if he ever tried to deceive them.

Unbeknownst to Ray, his crew decided to test the waters with the transaction going to Mexico.

Instead of sending authentic bills, Burkes's second in command decided to send some of the funny money as payment for a shipment of cocaine. It was procedure for the cartel to examine the bills when a large transaction took place. When the money was sent through a sophisticated x-ray machine, they discovered it was counterfeit. Instantly, the call went up the line to the high-ranking officials of the cartel. As one would expect, the decision to pay Burkes a visit was inevitable. Two weeks later, Michael called Alexis at work and invited her to dinner with Jasmine and the kids. He wanted to spend some time with her and catch up. Alexis really wanted to go, but she danced around the invitation because Ray had plans as well.

"Michael, I really appreciate the offer, but I may be working late this evening. Can I get a rain check?"

Michael was somewhat disappointed, yet he understood his little sister was paying her dues to climb the corporate ladder. "No problem, sis. Let's plan for next weekend."

After hurdling that obstacle, Alexis got off of work a few hours later. She hated lying to Michael, but she really wanted to spend the evening with Ray. She had a glow as she arrived home and prepared for a night on the town with her new and improved beau. As Ray entered the condo, he tried to hide the nervousness he was feeling after hearing what his sergeant at arms pulled with the cartel. Alexis was so excited about their evening of romance. She barely noticed Ray sweating, although the room temperature was set at a comfortable seventy degrees.

Desperately trying to convince himself he could fix the problem with the cartel, he focused his attention on Alexis. He pulled her close and softly whispered in her ear, "So are you ready to be swept off your feet, beautiful lady?"

Alexis melted like butter in his arms as she stared into his eyes responding like an innocent schoolgirl, "Oh yes!"

At that moment, Burkes seemed to have regained his swagger. Alexis gently kissed him and walked into the bedroom. Burkes walked to the bar to pour a drink when there was a knock at the door. When he heard the knock, his fears resurfaced. Before acknowledging the visitor, he went to a drawer in the chest and pulled out a black 9-mm pistol. As he approached the door, the knock turned into pounding. Before he could react, the door was kicked in and five men wearing black ski masks and armed with assault rifles stormed into the condo. Clearly, Ray knew they were sent to execute him. He hoped by standing his ground, the assailants wouldn't go further than his dead body and leave without harming Alexis. Therefore, he was prepared to stand in the middle of the living room and began shooting. When the door was kicked in, Alexis primped in the mirror perfecting her makeup for her hot date. Initially, she didn't have a clue to what was taking place. After hearing the commotion, naturally she began to run into the living area to investigate. After seeing a person's arm with an array of tattoos, and black gloves that tightly gripped a very large gun, she stopped short of the bedroom door so she wouldn't be noticed by one of the attackers. Instantly, she knew Ray was involved in something life threatening. She covered her mouth in efforts to muffle the sounds of panic. Her thoughts raced rapidly, "Should I do something to help him? Should I hide? Why is this happening? What will Michael think if he finds my body lifeless next to Ray? How did this all turn for the worse? God, please help me!"

Ray was about to be murdered and Alexis knew it. As she began to back away from the entry of the bedroom, Ray made a dash for their room. Their eyes met instantly as if it was scripted. It seemed God suspended time so they could have a proper departing. Her tears uttered, "Ray, I will always love you."

Amazingly, Ray interpreted her message like she verbalized it to soft music. In response, his eyes spoke to her, "Thank you for being an example of love I've never known. You've loved me when the world asked why. We will meet again!"

Both Burkes and Alexis understood the plan. She ran into the closet as Burkes turned to face his executioners. Ray's next move astonished his soon-to-be murderers. He placed the gun down and raised his hands in submission. Clearly, he was signaling this would not be a Mexican standoff. He had accepted his fate. However, he used that time to quickly confess his sins. As Ray closed his eyes to speak to God, one of the gunmen positioned the red beam on his forehead to complete the mission. Before pulling the trigger, his comrade shouted, "¡Espera! Deja que haga las paces con Dios."

After making his peace, he looked at the tactical team and lowered his hands and nodded, as if to say, "I'm ready." The next thing he felt before his spirit left his body was an array of bullets hitting his chest and head. In a split second, he was gone. With Burkes removed from this realm of life, the condo grew silent as the team exited.

With tears overflowing, Alexis hovered over Ray's lifeless body. She shouted, "Why, why Lord? Why him? Why now?"

Soon thereafter, tenants filled the hallway in terror after seeing the aftermath of Ray's murder. The police showed up and quickly determined homicide should be called to begin their investigation. Once the scene was secure and Alexis gave a preliminary statement to the authorities, a neighbor sympathetically took Alexis to her apartment where she called her family to tell them what happened. Unfortunately, Alexis had more than the loss of Ray to deal with. While the police searched the apartment for evidence, they discovered seven kilos of cocaine and fifty thousand dollars in cash in a chest in the corner of the walk-in closet. Alexis didn't know Ray stashed drugs and money in the chest. He told her it was a few valuables inside, and he wanted to keep it there because he knew it would be safe. She trusted him and never inquired to view the contents of the chest. Ironically, the contents of the chest became a major focal point of the investigation. Once the scene was in the wrap-up phase, the detectives assigned to the case took Alexis downtown. While she sat in the interrogating room for two hours without human interaction, she began to tremble in fear.

Eventually, two detectives entered the room and began the inquisition. "Ma'am, I understand what you've been through is frightening, but we need you to answer some questions to make sense of all of this. We understand there's a Michael Fletcher on the lease. What is his relationship to you?" While staring into space, Alexis timidly answered, "He's my brother." With intentions to rattle her, one the detectives returned with a series of questions, "How would you describe your brother's relationship with the victim? Were they in business together? Did they have a disagreement that led to the murder of Raymond Burkes? Was this a drug deal gone bad? Alexis was dumbfounded. However, she replied with a few questions of her own. "Drug deal? What are you talking about? My brother doesn't live with me, and he has never seen Ray a day in his life. He would never use or sell drugs! What does he have to do with this? His name is on the lease because he helped me get the place!" Sensing he was able to get under her skin, the experienced investigator walked over to Alexis and shouted, "Well, what about you and Burkes? Explain seven kilos and fifty thousand dollars in cash sitting in your closet."

After boldly defending her brother, Alexis found it difficult to defend herself as she answered, "I, I, I, don't know."

Before the detectives could go full throttle with their questioning, Michael showed up with an attorney to assist Alexis. When she saw a familiar face, she felt relieved. They were allowed into the interrogating room as the two sides exchanged pleasantries.

"Attorney Jacob Thomas and this is Michael Fletcher, the brother of the detainee. I will be providing Alexis with legal representation."

Since Michael's name was on the contract, the detectives elected to keep him in the room as well. "So Attorney Thomas, will you be representing both parties?" Michael looked concerned. "We have evidence that suggests the apartment, where the murder took place, doubled as a hub for the distribution of cocaine." Michael's mouth dropped as he looked at Alexis in shock!

"Wait a minute. Why am I in question?" Things began to heat up quickly.

"Michael, don't say a word! Are you formally charging any one of them with a crime?"

The lead detective responded arrogantly, "We can if you and your clients choose to play hardball. Consider this little sit down a courtesy, because to be honest, we have enough to hold Alexis since the apartment is her primary residence. So I strongly suggest somebody start talking. That's unless your attorney has better legal advice for you. You have five minutes to decide."

The detectives left the room, leaving the three of them to make a decision. "Alexis, I can't believe you! What have you done? Your selfish decisions now have us in this mess!"

"Michael, wait! Yelling at your sister will not solve anything. Now, they are going to walk in expecting to hear something worth listening too. We need to figure out what we can give them, so you two won't be charged with anything. Alexis, we need to know if you have any involvement in this other than dating Ray Burkes. I need to know everything in order to build a defense."

Alexis continued to feel nauseated as she scanned her brain for anything that could serve as a defense. "First of all I didn't have any involvement in Ray's affairs. I never questioned his goings and comings. I can't think of anything that can prove my innocence."

Michael sat and listened with disgust. "How could she had been so stupid to mess up her life for that dude? Lord, please help us!"

The lead detective returned with a cup of coffee in one hand and a stack of files in the other. This time, another well-dressed gentleman with an ID badge that read DEA accompanied him.

Even Attorney Thomas was intimidated by his presence. The room quickly filled with uncertainty. "Well, have you decided to give us anything to run with?"

Michael felt the need to take lead chair of their bewildered defense team. "Sir, I have no involvement at all in this matter. I am only a brother who wanted his sister to break free and start a new life without Burkes. I cosigned for her condo because I wanted to do my part to help her. My sister doesn't have anything to give you because I believe she truly didn't know what he was doing. She is the true definition of a hopeless romantic and it has led all of us here today. We will take a lie detector test tonight if we have to, but all we have is our word."

The DEA agent gave the detective a look that suggested he was about to end the conference. Before he began to speak, he reached for the folder that contained surveillance photos of Burkes and Alexis and created a make shift collage for them.

"I'm Agent Davis of the DEA. We have been tracking Burkes for some time now. We know when he approached you the day outside your building. We know how he used your home as a hub for his transactions. We did begin tracking your whereabouts and interactions with Burkes's outfit, and to be honest, we feel you indeed were unaware of his criminal ventures."

Alexis's eyes opened to a new world as she processed his words, "So are you saying you believe us?"

Agent Davis nodded and confirmed her interpretation, "Yes, we believe you and you all are free to go."

The defense team of Fletcher Thomas & Fletcher simultaneously took a much-needed sigh of relief. The HPD detective leaned back in his chair with his arms folded feeling he could have gotten something out of Alexis. It was a fair assumption that he didn't have the same agenda as Agent Davis. Playing the role of a trained skeptic, the detective arrogantly said, "I guess this is your lucky day."

Michael looked at him with confidence, "We don't believe in luck. Good night, detective."

As they walked out of what seemed to be Guantanamo Bay, Alexis couldn't hold back the desire to share her thoughts with Agent Davis. "Sir, I just have to tell you thank you. I know you may feel you were just doing your job and letting us go was strictly based on evidence you had in that folder. However, whether you know it or not, I feel you were sent by God to vindicate us. I don't know where you came from tonight, but I will rest knowing you were sent by God."

Agent Davis always considered himself a professional and didn't talk about his religious beliefs with anyone on the job, but Alexis hit an area that drained his professionalism like an emptied tub. As she spoke, he secretly understood why he was led to stop by the station as he returned home from a speaking engagement. Davis had no intentions on working the interrogation room on the Burkes's case; simply because, he had no idea Burkes had been murdered. He only stopped to pick up a file he needed for a meeting the next morning. Divine intervention further explained why he was running late for the engagement. Earlier he'd decided to take his government-issued vehicle that had the surveillance photos of Burkes tucked away in a box inside the trunk, instead of taking his personal car that sat in the garage with an empty gas tank. As he retraced his steps, he concluded God perfectly orchestrated his evening so he would be a blessing to someone in need. Davis's courteous, professional demeanor took a back seat as he spoke, "Alexis, I'm beginning to think you're right. To be honest, I never talk about God while I'm working. For years, I've felt I had to separate what I do for a living from my spiritual beliefs. Young lady, tonight you've taught me a valuable lesson. I now realize in everything I do, He is to accompany me. So let me thank you for being my angel tonight."

She began to tear up as they shook hands and eventually hugged.

Michael looked on as he stood near the water cooler replenishing his dehydrated body. He felt like he had gone twelve rounds in a heavyweight fight. The car ride from the precinct was a somber trip to say the least. Michael held back from saying anything malicious. Actually, he began to show signs of condolence toward his baby sister. When he thought of her relentless love for Burkes and how he himself viewed her as a hopeless romantic, he understood that when his sister says I love you, it's unconditional. Michael looked at Alexis as she leaned against the passenger side door with her head resting against the window. His heart filled with compassion for her as she wrestled with the loss of Burkes. He grabbed the steering wheel with his left hand and gently placed his right hand on her left leg. When Alexis felt the touch of her brother, she instantly turned to look at him in anticipation of his brotherly support as he so often provided.

"Lexi, it's going to be OK. I understand your heart and I want you to know I am not upset with you and I do forgive Ray."

As Jasmine remembered the toll that taxing experience had on the family, she also wondered what happened to that compassionate, understanding version of Michael Fletcher.

As her mind snapped back to their present issue concerning her brother, she felt Michael was being indifferent because it was her blood relative that needed a favor. The more she thought of his selfish ways, the more she secretly stored a small amount of distaste for him.

"Are you coming to bed or will you just sit over there and stare out the window?" Jasmine never responded as she sat with her back toward Michael. "Jasmine, Jasmine! Why are you being so bullheaded? My freaking goodness, I don't understand why you are acting like this." The more he talked, the more she wanted to put him out of his misery!

"You just don't get it, do you? You think your word is the final word. I guess that's partly my fault because for years, I've allowed you to be the one who gives the final approval. I have been a very good wife and I have a say in what goes on around here. Tomorrow, I am going to call my brother and tell him it's a go. Like you, I will do what I can to help my blood!"

When she completed the last sentence, Michael knew what held her in deep thought and caused her to skip dinner. "Oh, OK, there it is! I knew sooner or later the condo incident would come out."

Jasmine quickly rose to her feet and began to yell, "You act as if I've been waiting to throw things in your face. I never gave you that indication. I think you felt stupid for not listening to me when I tried telling you about Alexis and Ray! The problem is and has always been the fact that you want to be Mr. Perfect in your thinking and how you deal with people. The only reason I sat here and thought about Alexis, Ray's murder, and the whole incident you went through with the police is because it's funny how you went against your spiritual beliefs when it came to your precious baby sister."

Michael seemed to get upset as well, "Wait a minute. I did that to help her get away for Burkes!"

Jasmine countered Michael's swing like a prize-fighter. "If that's what you tell yourself to ease your spirit, go right ahead! You are a grown man. Surely, you knew Alexis was being evasive when we wanted to visit, never giving you the elevator code to get to her floor. How can you cosign for her condo and couldn't even get the elevator code? You want to know why? She didn't want you to ever come unannounced. You can't tell me you thought she was sitting all alone and Ray wasn't in the picture. I think you didn't want to come to that conclusion because that would mean you screwed up! That would mean Mr. Perfect aided in creating the ideal demon's den for lust and fornication. News flash Michael. That's exactly what you did and we both know how it turned out! What infuriates me more than anything is you went against your so-called better judgment because it was your sister!"

When Jasmine took the floor and began to unleash her frustrations, Michael sat at the edge of the bed with his head hanging down like a kid in the principal's office. Deep down inside, he knew Jasmine was hitting things on the head as if her words were being shot from a hunter's rifle with skilled precision.

As promised, Jasmine called Jason bright and early the next morning to give him the good news. Michael overheard her conversation as he poured a routine cup of caffeinated joe to jump-start his day. Although he didn't do a good job supporting his opinion, he continued to feel his position was valid. He saw a side of Jasmine he'd never seen before. He felt she was off base with accusations of compromising his beliefs for his sister. Nevertheless, in order to keep peace, he decided to leave it alone and prepared for Jason and Cynthia's arrival. After concluding her conversation with Jason, Jasmine entered the kitchen in a very good mood.

"Good morning, Fletch. How are you this morning?"

Michael restrained himself from sarcastically commenting on her renewed energy. Clearly, she was walking in victory lane from last night's overtime win.

"I'm good. You seem quite lively this morning. Was that Jason on the phone?"

Jasmine placed a bowl of oatmeal on the table and grabbed a spoon and a cup of orange juice from the counter. "Yeah, he was very happy we decided to let him and Cynn move in."

Michael couldn't help taking a cheap shot at the champ as he disagreed with her recollection of an unanimous decision for Jason's move. "Cynthia."

Jasmine looked up from her bowl of apple cinnamon oatmeal, "What?"

Losing his resolve to hold back his feelings, he responded, "Her name is Cynthia. When you said let him and Cynn move in, it kind of had a cursed ring to it."

It went back and forth like a match between Venus and Serena Williams. Jasmine had to catch herself and use a little conflict resolution she learned during the group dynamics seminar at work. "Oh, did I say it like that? Forgive me, Fletch. By all means, I definitely want to refrain from speaking curses into existence. Life and death is in the power of the tongue. Right?"

Michael knew Jasmine was being passive aggressive. He decided to walk out instead of responding. Michael had a very competitive nature and remaining in the kitchen would only increase the chances of his alpha male characteristics to resurface. As he walked out, Jasmine whispered to herself, "Is that apology good enough, Mr. Perfect?"

Chapter 3

. . . We Will Serve the Lord

Within weeks, the move from Ball Ground, Georgia, was complete. Brandon and Chris were happy to have their uncle around. Jason represented a male role model of a different sort for them. They absolutely loved their father. Their excitement wasn't out of desperation to be rescued from his tyranny. Jason was simply younger and shared some of the same energy when it came to sports, music, clothes, and definitely taste when it came to the ladies. Now that they were older, their swagger was beginning to take form and Uncle Jason was like the old guy from the beer commercials. To them, he was the most interesting man in the world. It didn't take long for Jason and Cynthia to settle into the day-to-day operation of their family's home. Michael didn't want to wait too long before they had a little sit down to discuss his concerns. Out of respect, Jasmine felt the least she could do was support Michael when they all got together. Even though they had their moments when they had differences in opinions, Jasmine knew Michael meant well. It was a Friday evening, and the four adults devoured a fabulous dinner. Cynthia was an excellent cook and she mesmerized everyone's taste buds with her crawfish etouffee.

"Cynn, that was delicious. You have to teach me how to make that!"

Michael looked at Jasmine, "Baby, stay in your lane. Stick to your famous chicken and shrimp Alfredo and I'll be happy. We'll let Cynthia handle the etouffee."

Jasmine threw her hand up, "Whatever!"

They all laughed as they leaned back in their chairs to make room for desert. Shortly thereafter, they decided to take the get together into the family room. Desert was served as the scheduled chat began.

"OK, guys, before we start, I want you to bite down on my famous apple pie with two scoops of vanilla ice cream!"

Truthfully, it wasn't actually Jasmine's pie. Michael just sat and laughed at her. "Babe, don't you mean Jasmine's famous store-bought pie?"

She always took credit for taking a mere frozen desert and heating it perfectly, thus giving it the home-made appearance. In her eyes, she was a part of the baking process. Jason and Cynthia sat on the sofa near the fireplace while Michael comfortably positioned himself in his favorite chair. Jasmine was a flexible woman and loved sitting on the floor during family time. Cynthia offered her seat to the lady of the house.

"Jasmine, you can sit here. I'll sit on the floor."

Jasmine kept scooping her pie and ice cream, "Girl, I'm fine right here. I used to do yoga three times a week. Trust me. I'm comfortable. I have my pie and ice cream. Life is good right now!"

The evening was pleasant and Michael didn't want the mood to change. "Well, guys, I just wanted to let you know where I am with you all moving in and give you the opportunity to express any concerns you may have."

Jason and Cynthia looked at each other with satisfied faces. Neither of them had any concerns. Jasmine took lead, "First of all, we are happy you guys are here. We want you to feel at home."

Michael nodded in agreement, as he resumed lead. "Jason, I know you are an outstanding young man and you have chosen a beautiful wife-to-be. I want to help you guys get situated as much as possible. But I'll admit it took some persuading when your request came down the wire. I just want to make sure we maintain certain spiritual standards in our home. I'll be lying if I said I wasn't concerned about you living out wedlock under our roof. Don't get me wrong. I'm glad you guys are here, but doing things the right way is important to me. As head of the house, it's my duty to consider how God views this situation."

Jason and Cynthia listened with informative ears. In order to have crystal clear clarity, Cynthia asked, "So are we talking about sex? Are you saying if we had sex that would be a problem?"

Jasmine stopped eating and awaited Michael's response. "Well, to be honest, Cynthia, that is a huge part of it. If you were married, I'd say knock yourself out, but you're not married and that's the problem."

Jason looked at his sister with a look that said, "Is he serious?" Jasmine felt bad because she didn't give her brother a head's up. Feeling caught in the middle, she decided to stay silent to mask support for Michael, although she didn't feel the same way he did. Jason chimed in, "Why wasn't that expressed before we moved here? I understand your view, but let's be real for a second. She is about to be my wife. Surely, you don't expect me stop having sex with her."

Michael answered somewhat passive aggressively, "Jason, do what you like, just not in my house."

Any visiting fly on the wall could tell the mood had changed and things were heating up a bit. Jason responded, "Wow, that's funny. You have definitely changed. You preaching now?"

Cynthia pulled Jason's arm to stop him from getting upset.

Michael asked for clarity, "So what does that supposed to mean?"

Jason leaned forward and looked at the Fletchers, "It means you had no problem having sex with Jasmine in my parents' home when you were only dating her. Do you remember that I slept in the room next to hers? Obviously, you didn't have the same convictions when you were just her boyfriend. Now, in all your wisdom, you lay out your expectations for us. You have a lot of nerve, Michael. Let's go baby! Oh, am I allowed to sleep in the bed with her? I don't want to violate your prearranged sleeping assignment and treat Cynthia like you did my sister."

As they walked toward the bedroom, Jasmine looked at Michael, "I guess that didn't go as planned. One day, you will learn to consider everything before you push your agenda."

As Jasmine left the room, Michael disregarded Jason's account of events and remained adamant about what he will allow in his house.

As they prepared for bed, Jason was upset with Michael's arrogance. "Did you notice how he spoke like he was on the throne? This is my sister's house too!"

Cynthia sat on the bed next to him and rubbed his back. "I know, but Jasmine didn't say a word. She never revealed how she felt. Do you think she supports Michael?"

As Jason listened to Cynthia, that could have been the case. "I don't know. It's funny how he acts as if he doesn't do any wrong. My sister thought he was the perfect man for her. After watching his mannerisms, I'd say he is obsessed with being superior in any situation. No wonder my nephews cling to me. Maybe they are relieved to know they won't be judged for every mistake they make."

Jason walked into the adjoining bathroom as Cynthia suggested he talk to Jasmine alone to see how she feels. The couple wanted to be realistic with Michael and Jasmine. They were young, vibrant, and sexually in tune with each other. Jason walked out of the restroom with his shirt off displaying his six-pack and chiseled torso. He was a former high school linebacker that led his team to a state championship and played two years for the Georgia Bulldogs before completely blowing out his knee. It was three years since he touched a collegiate field, yet his body looked as if he was ready for the NFL combines. He stayed in shape and Cynthia felt privileged to be the beneficiary of his affection. Cynthia looked at him as he looked in the drawer for a shirt to sleep in.

"You don't need a shirt. Get in this bed, boy!" Cynthia had that look in her eye.

"Girl, are you crazy or do you have amnesia? That man just arrogantly asked you not to defile his house by touching me. Lusting will not be tolerated! With all the music equipment he got, I wouldn't be surprised if the room is bugged with cameras and microphones."

She laughed, "Well, I'm going to touch and lust and whatever comes to mind. We'll just check for the cameras and microphones first. We will definitely have to find all the microphones because you are too vocal when I'm handling my business. You know, this may teach you to stop moaning from start to finish."

Jason's eyes were as big as beach balls as Cynthia stood with her hand on her curved hips. Her nightie fell short of her thighs and allowed her to reveal the legs of a salsa dancer. Cynthia was a well-built lady. She was approximately 5'8" and 155 pounds. Like her fiancée, she was toned and extremely beautiful. When she let her hair down, she looked like a Cajun version of Pocahontas. She was a native of Baton Rouge, Louisiana, and you knew it when she spoke with her seductive down south accent that would draw men from far and wide. Even though they were alone in the room, Jason felt embarrassed.

"OK, it was that one time. You act as if I consistently howl to the moon every time you touch me."

Cynthia was quick witted and loved having fun with her sweetie. She slowly walked to the window exaggerating her movement, so her backside would bounce like poetry in motion. This always caused him to slip into hypnosis. As Jason locked his sights on her captivating seduction, he found every step more alluring. She opened the blinds and pointed outside. "Well, it looks like a full moon tonight!"

Jason smiled, "You are a naughty little something. They say make sure you know everything about your mate before you marry them. I never knew you were this defiant."

Cynthia walked toward Jason as he sat on the bed, pushed him back, and straddled him. He always melted when she was enthusiastic about intimacy. Cynthia unwrapped her hair from the grandmother bun all women tend to style at bedtime. She intentionally made matters more tempting as she licked her lips and lowered her eyelids to barely expose her hazel eyes as her long hair fell perfectly into place. At that point, Jason began to lose all faculties. She slowly leaned over to nimble on his ear. At that point, his hormones were jumping like jungle monkeys from limb to limb in mass hysteria. Softly, she whispered, "Are you ready?"

By then, his eyes were closed, as he headed off to ecstasy. He was reduced to only being able to provide a slow satisfied nod. Suddenly, Cynthia said rapidly, "OK, good night. Make sure you say your prayers." She hopped off Jason and hid under the covers. Jason instantly sat upright and returned to reality.

"Whoa, whoa! What are you doing? Come on, baby!"

In a high-pitched humorous voice, Cynthia said, "Boy, bye! You heard what Reverend Michael said. I'm scared! You're not getting me in trouble because you can't control your monkeys!"

She laughed loudly and disappeared under the covers once again. Jason began to lie on his back and went into a deep stare as he watched the ceiling fan go round and round.

"Man, that's messed up. Oh, Jasmine and I are going to have a little talk. Woo, I can't have my heart racing like this every night. You know when I tell Reverend Mike what you did; he's going to condemn you to hell for tempting God's people!"

They started laughing, turned off the lamp, and retired for the evening with the "no sex" clause intact.

The next morning, the house welcomed the rays of sunlight as Jasmine cooked a grand breakfast. She thought it could ease the tension that concluded their Friday night. Michael left earlier to meet potential clients at the studio. He grabbed a microwavable sausage croissant and vanished before sunrise. Jason usually got out of bed before Cynthia. That morning, his uprising was motivated by the smell of his sister's bacon, eggs, and pancakes. He walked into the kitchen ready to dive in.

"Good morning, sis."

Jasmine turned around and removed another batch of eggs from the sizzling skillet. "Good morning. You must be starving if you are here already."

Jason looked at her and said, "Yeah, I'm starving all right. Sex starved! Dealing with that would make Jenny Craig eat a pound of bacon!"

They both got a kick out of that little icebreaker. "Did you wake up Cynn?"

Jason replied, "You mean Cynthia? 'Cause, she was too scared to be sin last night. Because of her and your preacher husband, I dreamt I was in a convent with a group of unattractive, mean, boring nuns. It was weird! I spent half the night trying to avoid getting hit with a ruler. When I woke up, I almost screamed, 'cause it wasn't much different from this house. See how your husband has taken my action from my real life and my dream life too?"

Jason had Jasmine rolling in laughter. "Boy, stop it! You have a joke for everything. I'm going to take you to open mic at the improv."

Cynthia finally woke up and walked into the dining area in good spirits. It's almost like they sensed Michael wasn't home. Jasmine felt they would eventually want to debrief after the meeting the night before. Jason felt like he was back in Ball Ground and his big sister was making sure he had a solid breakfast before his Pop Warner football games on Saturday afternoons. Needless to say, he felt they could talk about anything.

"Sis, can I ask you something?"

Jasmine premonition had surfaced. She answered as she placed dirty dishes into the dishwasher. "Sure, what's up?"

Cynthia began eating as Jason inquired, "I have always known Michael as an easygoing guy. After last night, he kinda sounded like a control freak. Be honest, are you happy?"

Jasmine attempted to derail her brother's curiosity. "Why are you asking me that, boy? That's my husband and we have a good family."

Jason knew Jasmine didn't want to appear to be against Michael. "Come on, sis. We've always been truthful with each other. Last night, it seemed like you wanted to say something, but you allowed Michael to take over. You've been a confident person your whole life. I've never seen you take a back seat to anyone. I got the feeling that he feels his word is final. Never once did he ask for you to express your position. So once again, are you happy with him?"

As her brother asked again, she thought of her husband's heart and his love for his family and God. "Yes, Jason, I am happy. We don't always see eye to eye, but he is a very good husband and father. I think he means well. He just doesn't know how to accept things that challenge his plan or philosophy."

Cynthia listened as the siblings talked. She digested the scrumptious breakfast and waited for an opportunity to join the chat. Jasmine continued, "I know you guys were caught off guard with his topic. Personally, I know you are going to have sex. Now, don't get me wrong. I don't recommend you have the knockdown, panting, I-need-a-cigarette version, especially if you like to make noise."

Cynthia looked at Jason with a burst of laughter that almost caused her to regurgitate her pancakes. Of course, Jason didn't find it amusing. Jasmine knew what caused Cynthia to almost lose it.

"What? My brother likes to express himself? Oh my goodness, that's good. Most men just give the animalistic bear growl and it's back to reality. Next thing you know, they are sleepier than a newborn after a warm bottle and a good burp."

Jason felt like a naked model in a female art class.

"Guys, just know I love my husband and I try to support him as much as I can. He wants the best for you two, and I do too for that matter. I just feel it's unrealistic to ask you guys not to get busy from time to time."

Cynthia appreciated Jasmine's honesty and replied, "Although it will be very hard to do, we want to respect the house rules. I know what Michael was trying to say and why. He just had a demanding way of saying it. I promise we will try to stay pure. Jason and I don't want to put you in a difficult situation with him."

Jason rolled his eyes as he looked at his sister. "I guess Cynn is going to need some of your moo-moo night gowns. I'm sure you have a collection of them so Rev. isn't tempted at night. If ya'll expect me to behave, Cynn will have to look like a grandmother before she gets into bed. Then again, I still may take granny around the block if she doesn't smell like liniment."

As usual, Jason had his audience engaged in cheer. Jasmine returned, "Boy, you missed your calling. You are silly! Now on a more serious note, I received a text this morning saying the construction company wants to meet with you and discuss employment."

Jason was a certified welder. After he told Jasmine he wanted a change of scenery and see what Houston had to offer, she began to network and see what could be done to get him a sit down with Hunter's Architectural Innovations. Jason was excited about the opportunity. If he lands the job, it would definitely help them get their own place a little quicker than originally planned. Cynthia was waiting for her results from the test she took to be a certified teacher in Texas. She left Georgia with two years' experience as a seventh grade Math teacher. She felt confident her scores would come back in her favor. She actually interviewed and was offered a teaching position. However, the job was contingent on passing the test. They planned to set a wedding date, once they found gainful employment. With the good news from his sister, Jason started to reconsider his brother-in-law's house rules. He replaced his comedy act with a more mature commentary, "You know maybe we should try to abstain from doing anything sexually and honor God's word. I mean, at the end of the day, we want a blessed marriage and doors of opportunities to open for us." Jasmine stopped rinsing the dishes and looked in shock, while Cynthia shared Jason's sentiments with newfound adoration for her prince.

Michael's day seemed to start with a bang as he met with the management group of one of the hottest up and coming hip-hop artists. The group bought a large amount of studio time and some of Michael's hottest tracks. When he offered to write the lyrics for the tracks he had sold them for an extra fee, they ultimately inked a deal for that as well. In total, Fletch had worked a contractual agreement worth 74,000 dollars to be paid over a three-month period. In addition, a second meeting was scheduled to sit down and discuss his percentages and royalties for writing some of the artist's material. Needless to say, his day was productive. It was the big break he was looking for. The studio was barely paying the bills and today justified all the sacrifices he'd made thus far. He couldn't wait to get home and share the good news with Jasmine. He thought about everything he's been through to get this opportunity. As he pulled into the driveway, Jason and Cynthia were leaving to go for their daily run. He blew the horn to get their attention and waved as they walked toward the nature trail. It was difficult to determine if Michael greeted them with a wave to ease the tension or because he was in such a good mood that he would have greeted anybody walking near his home.

Jason looked at Cynthia and said, "What do you think he has up his sleeve now?"

Cynthia shrugged her shoulders, "Who knows. Whatever it is, we are going to enjoy our day. Now, let me see you sweat, boy!"

Jason felt the urge to tease her in retaliation for the stunt she pulled in the bedroom. He pulled off his shirt exposing his ripped upper body and huge arms and placed his headphones on his ears. He then gave the patented L.L. Cool J lick of his lips and replied, "You sure you'll be able to stay focused when I start sweating?"

She punched him in the arm and struck back, "Just make sure you run with me or ahead of me. If you run behind, you're not exercising. You'll just be pacing yourself to look at my booty!"

Meanwhile, Jasmine was gathering the clothes that were to go to the cleaners when Michael walked in. She knew something good went on at the studio. He was an easy read as he walked in smiling from ear to ear.

"What's up, babe? Come give your man a kiss."

Jasmine walked out of the closet looking at him with curious eyes. "Hey, Fletch. Why are you so bubbly?"

He sat on the bed and took off his shoes and explained. "Well, your man just inked a nice deal. I mean it's not a multimillion dollar deal, but it is the biggest I've had at one time. If I play my cards right, it could blow up into something bigger."

Jasmine was excited for Michael. She prayed for an opportunity to open up for him. "So how much are we talking?"

Michael confidently answered, "Seventy-four grand! That doesn't include royalties I will be making for writing the lyrics for the tracks I sold them. I am going to meet with the management group and record label to discuss the numbers. This could be my big break! After church tomorrow, I'm treating everybody to lunch."

Jasmine liked that idea and added, "And a little shopping at the Galleria?"

Michael laughed, "Yes, babe, and a little shopping at the Galleria. When are the boys coming home?"

Jasmine replied, "They went to a birthday party. They should be here around seven or eight."

Michael wanted to share the news with them in person. Later that evening, the boys returned, and Michael couldn't wait to break the news. He knew they would be excited for him, but even more excited when he told them whom he was going to be working with. Quite naturally, they were musically inclined and loved hip-hop. Michael nonchalantly brought up music and whom he thought was overrated in the world of hip-hop. He knew that would spark a conversation with the boys. Jasmine knew exactly what he was doing and added a few logs to the fire to intensify the buildup. On the contrary, Jason and Cynthia didn't have a clue to what Michael was doing. However, they jumped in the conversation strictly out of love for the hip-hop culture. Jason through in his two cents, "Personally, I feel Biggie is the best. Definitely head and shoulders above Tupac."

Cynthia hurried to sip some of her soda to respond. "Hold up! Now don't compare anybody to my Tupac, because that was one sexy black man!"

Jason gave her a crazy look, "We are not talking about who looks a certain way. We are talking about the music. When it comes to who has the smoothest delivery and swag, it's Biggie hands down. Now, you are just lusting, and you were asked last night not to do that."

Michael and Jasmine put their head down and chuckled. Knowing Jason was a shade tree comedian, she didn't return fire. Cynn simply responded by clapping her hands and saying, "Oh, now that's a good one. I'll save mine for later."

Jason knew what that meant. Tonight, she was going to tease him with her Beyoncé's *Crazy Love* bounce until he passed out. Quickly, he tried to make a truce. "Come on, baby, I was just playing."

Chris gave his opinion. "There's nobody doing it like Drake. He can sing and he has the delivery Uncle Jason was talking about."

Michael asked Brandon what he thought. "I like this new kid people are feeling right now. Busy Bee is an artist that gives straight lyrics without the cursing and degrading people. To me, he's like a Rakim, but with that new flavor. He has the lyrical skills and swag to get people to hear what he's saying instead of filling the track with stupid hooks repeated three hundred times."

Chris quickly interrupted, "Oh yeah, I forgot about that boy, Busy Bee. Yeah, he's for real."

Jason laughed, "Brandon, what you know about Eric B and Rakim?"

Michael knew it was the perfect time to break the news to the boys. Before he revealed his secret, Jasmine had something to say. "Wait a minute, what about me?"

Chris looked at her like she was a country singer who grew up pumping the sounds of Dolly Parton and Hank Williams. Jasmine noticed his ridiculous expression and continued, "Boy, I had my favorites. I liked the Fat Boys. I remember trying to beat box on the bus while my friend Lisa tried to rap like Salt-N-Pepa, which is another one of my favorite groups."

When she finished, Chris nodded in agreement, "OK, Mom, I see ya!"

Jasmine felt proud to have respect from the gurus of rap city. Michael couldn't hold out any longer. "Well, guys, today was a very good day for your dad. I had a meeting with some potential clients and not only did they buy studio time, they bought some of my tracks and hired me as a writer for the project. That means, I will be working closely with your boy, Busy Bee!"

Their eyes lit up like a Christmas tree.

"You're what?" Brandon shouted.

Chris scrambled for his phone to send a tweet. "Oh, I'm about to be a trending topic!"

Michael interrupted the transmission, "Whoa, not too fast. Don't tell anybody. This is a business and we must be mindful that artists and record labels frown upon media leaks and things like that. You'll get your time to stunt with pictures from the recording sessions as I build a working relationship with the kid."

Even Jason was excited about the project. "Michael, when you meet with them, ask if he has a security team."

Cynn looked at him and rolled her eyes. "Last time I checked, you were a welder. What, you plan on melting people that run on stage?"

This time, Brandon and Chris got a kick out of that one. Brandon added, "Man, that's cold. You can't burn people, Unc!"

Chris leaned back in his chair cracking up as he held his stomach and said, "Yeah, Uncle Jason, I can see you out there dropping people like it's hot. You might want to leave the security gig alone!"

Even Jason had to giggle with that one. "Boy, I'll tell ya, family members are the worst critics."

The next morning, everyone got dressed for church. Before long, they all sat on the fourth row, centered with the pulpit. After the offering plate was passed around and the choir sang, the minister was on his way up to preach. Pastor Dixon was a tall man in stature. In addition, he had a way to draw people with his message from God. His smile and sincerity gave people insight to what it looks like to have the spirit of God dwelling within. He was very accessible for the young, as well as the old. The Fletchers joined the church when Brandon was two years old. Therefore, the fourth row was known as Fletcher row. While they downplayed their popularity in the church, they were used many times as an example in Pastor Dixon's sermons. He was proud to have members like the Fletchers. He felt they were a fine representation of a godly family.

Pastor Dixon greeted the church in his customary way and began the lesson: "Today, I want to talk about trusting God in unfamiliar territory. The title of the sermon is *The Miracle is in Your First Step*. The story of Jesus walking on water will always be a trending topic. However, today we won't focus on how Jesus confused scientific theory. While it was amazing for Him to do so, the lesson didn't take shape until Peter stepped out of the boat. Somebody here may ask what is so significant about Peter's decision to step out onto the water. In Matthew 14:28–29, 'And Peter answered him and said, Lord, if it be thou, bid me come unto thee on the water. And HE said, Come.' I want to stop right there. I'm sure Peter wanted Jesus to understand not to call him out there if he couldn't make good on that miracle."

The congregation laughed as Pastor Dixon always held their attention with well-placed humor. Jason thought, "Okay, I think this lesson is for me."

The Pastor continued, "That suggests to me that Peter was curious to see if Jesus could bless him to do something supernatural as well. Is it fair to say Peter's curiosity created a boldness to try God? As I attempt to dissect Jesus's response, I conclude that he didn't have a problem with Peter's curiosity or boldness to test His power. Notice in this text, HE didn't hesitate to reply to Peter. With extreme confidence in what

HE could do, He simply said, 'Come.' If my interpretation is correct, are we lacking a certain boldness to simply try God? Are we too comfortable in our inabilities? Is living in mediocrity safer than trusting God to live a water walking lifestyle? Does our fear of the unknown keep us tucked away in our comfort zones? Let me stop before people walk out of church angry with me. Let's get back to Peter and the first step. Now, the first step for Peter was a blessed step or an awakening for him, because with the first step, he found things were not as bad as his fears advertised. The first step could definitely be considered the faith step. How many of us were in a destitute situation, and when we made up our mind to just step, we saw God and his power in ways that caused us to throw up our hands in praise? How long will you go before you say, 'Enough is enough.' When will you say, 'I want to see what the buzz is about with this Jesus character.' Think about this. If the power to walk on water was a product Jesus bottled up and sold on television, I'm sure he would have a money back guarantee for the nonbelievers. I also know it wouldn't be a need to staff a department of customer service reps, because the phones wouldn't ring! You tell me who in their right mind would want a refund after seeing how good God is? Who would want a refund on blessings for generations, peace, joy, love, grace, and mercy and a free membership into heaven? From the bible, I also infer. Peter became confident in walking supernaturally as long as he focused on Jesus. Nothing else mattered. He walked on water like he was made for it, floated upright like a well-constructed yacht. How many of you are focused on God and enjoying the wind at your backs while your haters watch you do the impossible?"

The organist began to run his fingers up and down the scale, providing a melodic buildup as Pastor Dixon preached. Michael began to cry. Although he was the man of the house and the family's strong tower, he was reduced in God's presence. Likewise, Jasmine stood to her feet, clapped her hands. Tears began to trickle down her face as well. The boys also stood to their feet. The youth had their own section in the balcony. Brandon noticed the excitement many of his classmates had on their faces as the youth section looked more like a pep rally for Jesus! He looked at Michael, pointed to the balcony, and said, "I'm going up!" Chris joined his brother and in a flash they were a part of the party up top! Cynthia held Jason's hand tightly and stared into his eyes communicating, "Woo, God is awesome!"

Pastor Dixon paused and smiled as he walked toward the front pew. The camera panned over and it showed Sister Madison on the church's big screen pretending to hit the stress notes played by the organist with her eyes closed and full of joy! Pastor Dixon acknowledged her and shouted, "Play it Sister Madison! Play it!" The church roared again! Needless to say, they were getting their praise on! After the brief intermission, the congregation's roar lowered to an excited simmer to respectfully allow their pastor to provide more insight from the encounter on the water.

Pastor Dixon wiped his face with a handkerchief and class resumed: "OK, OK, calm down. You're causing me to have too much fun this morning. This may be too much for our first time visitors. I'm telling y'all now; Satan doesn't appreciate what you're doing. I mean he hates for anyone to praise God. I imagine him letting the old folks praise him a little bit, but he gets upset when the young people are determined to take the first step! Like Peter, our young people will soon discover that God actually keeps his promise. What a world we would have if the younger generation would fall in love with the first step. Some of them are way too hyper to walk. I see flocks and flocks of our youth running on water to Jesus! As we get back to the lesson, the story goes on to teach us that Satan will not sit by and let you enjoy your breakthrough without adversity. The second you step out of your circumstance and find yourself walking on water, he is plotting to send fearful situations to cause you to take your eyes off God! Somebody in this sanctuary finally got over their spouse walking out on them. You are at peace with the rejection, because now you've found true acceptance from the Lord. Yet before you can actually meet Jesus out on the water, in the midst of putting the wind to your back, Satan is now attacking your children. They want to live their own lives while living in your house. All of a sudden, they need freedom. They think their so-called friends understand them better than you after all the years you provided food, shelter, and love. Your job is laying off and your department is the first to go. I say this loud and clear, we have a word from God that tells us plainly; do not focus on that mess. KEEP YOUR EYES ON HIM! For if that were not the desired message, why would the bible give account of Peter sinking after he took his eyes off God? The problems Peter encountered on the water weren't by accident. It is always the design of the devil to convince you things around you will destroy you. I like to call it perfectly placed fear. Peter made the mistake of taking his eyes off God. I want to break that down. Here, a man decided to try God and began to do superhuman things. Yet when Satan used worldly issues to challenge his superhuman progress, he abandoned the supernatural gift to bow in fear to issues his faith had lifted him above. Clearly, his inability to focus on Jesus in adversity almost cost him his life. What is the message here in the book of Matthew? First and foremost, simply take the first step and watch God sustain you in ways you never thought was possible. Secondly, be aware of Satan's plot to interrupt your faith walk. Purposely choose to focus on Jesus, even when your problems threaten to consume you. If you focus on the Savior and place the wave under your feet. I'm sure the world will call you a surfer. You will become one who has the gift to balance in an unbalanced situation, the one who can take what was meant to destroy them, stand on top, and ride it until it scatters like a wave when it hits shore. Every surfer's goal is to ride a wave until they make it safely to the shoreline. Isn't it ironic that it's the same when you're experiencing the waves of life and when you reach your destiny the problem dissipates? I mean when you look back at that thing, you wonder why were you afraid of a problem that never had the ability to destroy you. Today, I declare you are a surfer. I confess as God's people, we will take the first step like Peter. We will focus on the one who was nailed to an old rugged cross and now stands at the end of our pain, at the end of our despair, the one who is simply saying, 'Come.' I can hear Jesus say right now, 'Look into my eyes and walk this way!' I see him with outstretched hands as he holds joy, peace, unconditional love, mercy, and grace. The final message from this story is if you just take the first step and persevere, your faith will be rewarded! For as a man of God and leader of this great church, I boldly declare for me and my people, 'In this house, we will serve the Lord!'"

When Pastor Dixon concluded, there wasn't a dry tear in the house. The message from God was loud and crystal clear. Jasmine held Michael's hand like it was their first date. Jason and Cynthia's resolve to abstain from premarital sex was strengthen. Furthermore, they realized Rev. Michael wasn't the tyrant he appeared to be. He just refused to take his eyes off God and actually helped them refocus so they can take the first step together.

Chapter 4

. . . Leaving a Comfort Zone

The weekend was over and it was back to work for the Fletchers. The kids prepared for school and Jason prepped for his interview with Hunter's Architectural Innovations. Cynthia planned on looking for a job until she got her scores in. Still impacted from the church service, every member in the house had smiles on their faces and greeted each other with love as they prepared for the day. Michael planned on getting in the studio and writing rough drafts ahead of time for the project. Jasmine had meetings all day and expected to work late. The boys had a typical day at school ahead of them. Afterward, Brandon planned on going to the volleyball game at the senior high and hang out with friends while Chris had football practice. Before long, the house was empty as their paths varied like airplanes leaving George Bush Intercontinental Airport. Jason arrived early for his interview ready to impress his potential employers.

Although he was a funny guy, he had another side. When it came to making money and selling himself, he easily switched to business mode. He was very confident in his abilities and he prayed things would go extremely well. Even though Jasmine put in a word for him, he refused to walk in thinking it was a done deal. Jason was a competitor and he wanted people to see him as Jason Carver and not Jasmine Fletcher's brother. He sat in the waiting area, pulled out his phone to Google Matthew 14:28, as he mentally repeated, "Take the first step!" Midway into the search, the receptionist called his name. He quickly looked up and approached the desk. "Mr. Carver, you can go to the conference room now. It's three doors down to your left." Jason clutched his folder of recommendation letters, thanked the receptionist, and walked to the conference room. Before walking in, he focused his spiritual eyes on Jesus and the winds of nervousness dissipated. He entered the room like a business executive. Ironically, it was the same room his sister made her first power move and accepted Michael's hand in marriage.

"Good morning, Mr. Carver. I'm Jim Morales. We would like to thank you for meeting with us this morning. As you may know, you were highly recommended by Stevenson Engineering and we respect their company a great deal. Obviously, someone considers you to be a great candidate for what we do here at Hunter's Architectural Innovations. We understand you have a wealth of experience as a welder. As we do all of our candidates, we did a preliminary work-related background on you and we too were impressed with what your former employers had to say. As you may know, there is a position we need to fill for a project that's underway and we feel your welding skills are definitely needed. So we are prepared to offer you the position."

Jason sat and listened with a very proud look. He wondered at what point he would have to sell himself to his interviewer. However, it wasn't necessary. It was more like the recruitment process he went through for his football scholarship. After realizing he had the job, he inquired, "I truly feel it's an honor to be considered for the position. However, before I accept, can you guys tell me what the position pays?" While it didn't show on his face, Jason hoped he wasn't out of line to jump directly to compensation.

Mr. Morales replied, "Oh, I apologize, by all means. Here at Hunter's Architectural Innovations, we consider every position a professional position; therefore, we have an offer sheet for you to review. If indeed you find the offer generous, feel free to sign and we will start the rest of the paperwork."

Jason read the offer sheet. Inside, fireworks went off like the fourth of July. On the exterior, he smiled and responded, "Yes, it appears we can now complete the remaining paperwork." Both were satisfied with the meeting and Jason left as an official employee.

Meanwhile, Michael worked at a feverish pitch to complete two songs for Busy Bee's project. When it came to music, he was a true workaholic. As he read through the rough draft, the phone rang. It was

Busy Bee's manager checking in to set up the meeting with the record label. He had good news and bad news for Michael.

"I wanted to touch base with you and tell you the meeting has been set to take place in two weeks. I know we thought it would be in a month or so, but the label wanted to speed up the process and get the ball rolling. Secondly, how you feel about working out in LA for a few months?"

That question threw Michael off because he assumed their artist would be working out of his studio in Houston. Michael returned, "To be honest, I don't know how to feel. I thought we had a deal to work out of my studio."

Mr. Johnson replied, "Well, Michael, this industry has levels of hierarchy and we have to do what the label allows. Once those guys go into a room, things change. The guy that originally signed off on the project to take place in Texas has been reassigned. The lady they have in place now is a west coast girl and she wants to oversee the project. Therefore, Los Angeles has become the new venue. We realize we are under contract with you and we will honor the 74,000 dollars we agreed on for the studio time."

Michael wasn't necessarily pleased with the news from Mr. Johnson. He quickly had a flashback of the last opportunity to work with the Crawford Boys in Nashville. What would happen if he passed on this opportunity as well? Could he leave his family for months in pursuit of his career? Anxiety seemed to build inside. After the phone call, Michael sat in deep thought, "Is this my test to step out of the boat? Man, I received the word yesterday, but I had no idea I would have to apply it this soon." He failed to realize God's timing is unpredictable. Many times, there is long-suffering for a breakthrough. While in other instances, God is swift with his blessings and we are left to scramble for baskets to hold his goodness. Fletch was given the distinguished duty to gather his baskets and yet he seemed to be somewhat apprehensive. He knew once he shared the information with Jasmine, his bearings would be set on course. She served as the rational risk-taker in the family. She had a way of setting goals and knocking down walls to get what she wants. Michael always admired her drive. He decided to end his writing session, especially after Johnson's phone call caused him to come down with the dreaded case of writer's block.

Jasmine stopped by the store to grab a few things and ran into her best friend. They were so close, people thought they were sisters. Jasmine asked, "So, Ms. Paige, what have you been up too?"

Standing with one hand on her shopping cart and the other on her hip, she answered, "Just working. I am up to my eyeballs in paperwork and traveling on business. I was just telling myself I have to start making time for me! I am going to Detroit on business next week. When I get back, I will start Team Paige."

Jasmine look puzzled. "Now what exactly is Team Paige?"

In a self-assured voice, she answered, "Girl, that's what I call my social circle. It will consist of me, myself, and I. One day out of the week, I will do what I want, when I want, and with whom I want."

Jasmine laughed and playfully slapped her hand, "Now that's enough! I agree with the first two. I don't know about the last one."

Paige laughed as well. "Girl, you know what I'm trying to say."

They continued to talk for a bit before completing the task of gathering groceries. They both vowed to make time and go out for lunch and catch up. By the time Jasmine got home, Michael and the boys were standing in the driveway arguing about who had a better overall game, LeBron James or Kevin Durant. Before getting out of the car she knew she would be thrown into the debate. Therefore, she listened as she pulled into the garage and gathered her thoughts. Brandon said, "Mom, come talk to your husband. He's saying LeBron is better than Kevin Durant and I'm getting irritated. Durant is clearly one of the best shooters in NBA history."

Michael couldn't take anymore of Brandon's novice analysis. "Okay, I'll give you that, but LeBron is a scorer and a defender. He controls the game with his ability to draw double teams and find his teammates. Durant shoots jumpers with an occasional drive for a dunk. LeBron scores in all kinds of ways. He's a bull when he attacks the rim and he runs the floor like an NFL receiver. Son, what are you thinking about?"

Jasmine felt it was time to end the conversation. "Okay, both of you have made your point. However, the best in my opinion is Kobe. He has more rings and you could argue he was good as Michael Jordan." She then turned and walked into the house with her hands up. "I'm just saying."

Chris laughed, "I'm with you, Big Mom! I think they forgot about the black mamba." To Jasmine's surprise, Cynn had dinner prepared and the table set. Jason was just getting out of the shower and couldn't wait to share the good news with Michael and his sister over dinner.

"Cynn, it smells like a Cajun kitchen in here. Oh my goodness, I can get used to this! What's on the menu?"

Cynthia responded, "Well, tonight, we will start with a nice salad and warm garlic bread. For the entrée, we will have items from the blackened side of the menu. First, you have your perfectly seared salmon. Next, your taste buds will dance when you consume my medley of blackened shrimp, scallops, and crawfish tails all served over a bed of my family's famous homemade jambalaya rice. Let's not forget the assortment of sauces to enhance your experience here at *Cynthia Boudreaux's Cajun Creations*."

They both laughed and gave each other a high five before Jasmine added, "While you are playing, you may have a double career as an educator and restaurant owner. You are multitalented and I can see you being extraordinary at both careers!"

Before long, the entire family was in full stride as their taste buds raced through the menu. Brandon was built like a slender basketball player but ate like a sumo wrestler. He demolished anything that sat in front of him. Things almost got testy between siblings over the warm garlic bread that served as a meal by itself, as both Brandon and Chris dipped it into the array of sauces. Jason allowed the family to settle into their meal before breaking the news.

"Guys, guess what? I got the job today! It was more like a recruitment visit than a job interview. They were impressed with my work as a welder and treated me with absolute professionalism. Jasmine, I want to thank you for helping me. I am very grateful!"

Jasmine was proud of her little brother. She knew he would do a great job in the interview room. Michael was excited for Jason as well. He always saw the potential in his brother-in-law. He then turned his thoughts on his dilemma. He didn't know whether to talk to Jasmine alone about the LA thing or present the proposal to the panel of family members. Ultimately, he decided to lay it on the table and hear what everyone had to say.

"Well, I guess this is a good time to tell you all about my day. Got a call from Busy Bee's manager and there has been a change in production venues." Jasmine's energetic chewing slowed to a snail's pace.

"The label has changed leads on his project and the new shot caller is from the west coast and wants to monitor the project from start to finish. Needless to say, she wants to be closer to her roots, so the project will be recorded in Los Angeles, which means if I stay on board, I will have to be there as well. Johnson said it would be a couple of months. In the record business, that means six to eight months, if things run smoothly."

Brandon and Chris looked stunned. "What about our games? You've never missed a game," Chris exclaimed.

Michael answered, "I understand, son. That's why I'm bringing it up while we are all here. They will still honor the contract for the studio time they've purchased. I didn't see this coming, and to be honest, I need some feedback from you guys."

Jasmine wanted Michael to express his concerns. "Instead of hearing what we think, let's hear why you are unsure about taking advantage of this opportunity."

Michael wasn't expecting that response from his wife. Yet he understood her reason for asking. "I don't know why I'm a little apprehensive. Maybe it's leaving you guys. I know that sounds minor, but it's a big deal to me."

The boys realized the pressure they'd began to put on their dad and attempted to reassure him. Brandon responded, "Dad, we will miss you too, but this is your opportunity to live your dreams. You've worked hard to get this chance. You can't leave it on the table. What's going to happen when I get a scholarship to play basketball in another state? Should I think about turning it down because I will miss my family?"

Chris tag teamed with his brother and added, "Yeah, Dad, it seems like Jesus is trying to bless you and you are afraid to step out of the boat. Don't worry about us. It's not like you are going away for ten years."

Jasmine smiled as she witnessed the spiritual maturity her boys displayed to encourage their father. Likewise, Michael felt like he was listening to his parents as his children urged him to apply God's word to this situation. Jasmine looked at Fletch and said, "Well, I guess you've got your confirmation to leave your comfort zone."

Jason placed his hand on his brother-in-law's shoulder, "Yeah, big fella, it's time to surf. Now, I mean that spiritually not literally. Don't get out there and try to surf for real and come back with one leg. It's real sharks in that water."

The dining room filled with giggles as the shade tree comedian added his punch line. After talking with the family, Michael felt empowered that leaving his comfort zone would yield supernatural blessings for him and his family.

Chapter 5

. . . The First Step

Although he didn't meet the executive that changed the production venue, Michael's meeting in California went extremely well. His apprehension subsided and ironically, a glimmer of excitement began to show by the time he flew back home to bid his farewells to his family. A month seemed to fly by like days and it was time to leave the boat. Michael opened his eyes to the sound of an extremely loud alarm clock. He reached out to hit any button he could get his fingers on. Jasmine was motionless in a deep sleep, as he continued to lie with his head under his pillow. It was three o'clock in the morning and he had a direct flight to Los Angeles scheduled to depart at seven. It was time to rise and get going. He took a deep breath, turned on his lamp, and whispered to himself, "All right, Fletcher, let's go." Minutes later, Jasmine rolled over and opened her eyes to her husband trying to find the match to his sock. She placed her hands under her head and looked at her man prepare to step out on faith.

"Need some help?"

Fletch looked up and said, "Oh, did I wake
you?"

She got out of bed, walked to a basket of folded
clothes, and instantly found the match.

"Wow, can you come to California every morning and help me start my day?"

She kissed him on the cheek. "Sweetheart, I
wish I could."

Before long, he was ready to bring his Texas way
of life to the west coast. Brandon and Chris served as
loving bellhops as they took their dad's bags to the car.
The ride to the airport was an upbeat trip. However,
when they stopped in front of the departure drop-
off, emotions resurfaced for the entire Fletcher family. The boys were in complete tears as they got out of
the car and held on to their dad for dear life. Jasmine
wanted to doll up for Michael, but she knew once it
was time to say goodbye, her makeup would competitively race her tears down her face and leave her
looking like a circus clown. She stood and looked up
into his eyes trying to wipe every tear he produced.

"I love you, Michael Fletcher. You show them
exactly who you are!" That was all she could manage to say before bursting into tears and burying her
head into his chest. It was a very heartrending scene.
Everyone that walked in and out of the airport knew
this was indeed a family! They finally managed to
say their goodbyes and Michael blended in with the

morning travelers as he entered the terminal. A few hours later, the plane safely landed at LAX. Michael had awakened from a twenty-minute power nap and gathered his thoughts while the aircraft taxied to the terminal. Before he stepped off the plane, he envisioned Peter's foot lifting out of the boat and stepping out onto the sea. He took a deep breath and said, "All right, Lord, with eyes on you, I'm ready to walk on water!"

Back in Houston, Jasmine and the boys were able to corral their emotions and start their week. Jason was on location of his new worksite. He met with various leads like the construction foreman, the electrician, and of course the lead welder. Cynthia had received her scores and was set for an interview for a teaching position. She was a shoe in, but she still had to go through the formalities. Jasmine didn't know how to feel, Michael was gone, and her brother and future sister-in-law were establishing themselves much quicker than expected. This meant it was a matter of time before they moved out and the adult interaction will have to come from elsewhere. Jasmine was very assertive when it came to her career, but she loved to be courted by her man. She was a devoted woman who gave everything to the man she loved. She could never love two men. It is fair to say she was a throwback. Her beliefs resembled women from the 1900s, when they were totally supportive of their mate no matter how tough times were, times when the men went off to war and the women worked in the factories to support. However, they kept the ability to be sensual, ego-stroking women that had a fresh apple pie and a romantic kiss waiting for their hero's return. Unfortunately, in today's society, the mentality of people has changed. She always criticized women who married for money or walked away from a marriage because struggling was an everyday occurrence. She had the kind of heart that flourished when it was nurtured with love. If you were a fan of someone like Jasmine, you would feel she deserves the "Wife of the Year" award. On the other hand, skeptics would want to see how she handles the absence of Michael's affection.

Fifteen hundred miles away, Michael had a driver standing near baggage claim holding a white piece of paper with his name written on it. He felt important as he introduced himself to the gentleman.

"Hello, I'm Michael Fletcher."

The two guys shook hands, gathered Fletcher's luggage, and went to the limousine parked in front of the terminal.

"Wow, this is big time! A limo just for me? Not bad for a first step."

He was taken to the label's head office to meet the execs. His entire day consisted of meet and greets, getting the keys to his office and apartment. Later on, he had a business dinner with Busy Bee and his management team. Needless to say, his itinerary was jam-packed. As the limo moseyed through the city, Michael read the street signs like a true tourist. Inside, he marveled at landmarks he'd only come to know through the movies. The driver seemed to get a kick

out of Michael's boyhood excitement, as he slowed
down, so Fletcher could soak it all in. His meeting
during his previous trip to Los Angeles with the label
was held offsite. Therefore, this was going to be his
first glance at headquarters. He would soon discover
the head office was a mere eight-minute walk from
the Staples Center. The limo rode past the palace
that housed Kobe Bryant's throne. Thinking about
Kobe and the Staples Center made him think about
Jasmine. He looked out of the window and smiled as
he remembered the night in the driveway when they
debated the best player in the league. Two minutes
later, the limo pulled in front of the office building.

"You mean to tell me the Staples Center is down
the street from headquarters? Brandon and Chris are
going to love this!"

The chauffeur placed the car in park, got out,
and opened the door for Michael.

"Have a great stay in Los Angeles, Mr. Fletcher.
I've been instructed to deliver your bags to your
apartment."

Michael thanked the gentleman and offered a
tip. He confidently walked into the building. Before
reaching the receptionist, he was greeted by Mr.
Johnson and an attractive young lady who seemed to
walk with a certain moxie. Instantly, he figured this
was the young lady who derailed the project from
being recorded in Houston. Michael secretly admitted she was astonishing as he noticed her perfect
curves that were accented by a sexy, yet professional
skirt and white blouse with small baby blue polka

dots that complimented her bronze skin. Her complexion was flawless. Her facial bone structure would make supermodels envious. Her ability to command attention was amazing, even while sporting a basic ponytail and black-framed glasses. Clearly, she didn't have to spend hours in the mirror to transform from pretty to stunning. Michael wondered if he would have to deal with her arrogance.

"Good morning! I am Tracy Sprewell and welcome to Los Angeles. As you know this is Mr. Johnson and we look forward to working with you on this project."

Likewise, Michael extended his hand to Tracy. "Good morning! It's a pleasure to be here and I also look forward to getting started."

As they walked to the elevators, Tracy took a mental note of Michael's height and manly presence. Her observation mirrored Michael's sentiments, as she secretly appreciated his attractiveness and alluring scent from his cologne. Once the elevator reached the forty-seventh floor, the doors opened and Michael was exposed to the immaculate décor of the executive level. He felt like he was walking into a Greek palace. Hand-carved marble columns complimented the travertine floors. Perfectly placed greenery accented an array of statues of Greek Mythical Gods. It seemed he had taken a trip to Greece instead of California. Huge windows allowed the entire floor to welcome the glow of sunlight. The layout provided a very inspiring ambience for the most unmotivated employee. If your desk sat on the forty-seventh floor, it was very difficult to have a case of the *Monday Blues.* Inspiration spewed from the decorations. Needless to say, to have a theme for the floor wasn't an accident. The big wigs understood a record label's creativity was essential for success. Michael felt his creative juices come alive as he made his way to Ms. Sprewell's office. He wondered if he would be fortunate enough to have a spot in Greece to work on Busy's project. They entered her office and she began to speak, "Mr. Fletcher, we have taken the liberty of setting up your office. Once we are finished with our little chat, my assistant will escort you to your cubbyhole."

Michael didn't necessarily like the word cubbyhole, because he didn't remember seeing anything that resembled a cubbyhole when he walked through Greece. He wanted an office in the mythical world on the forty-seventh floor, not some dreaded dungeon that once housed the likes of Medusa. He had no reason to believe he would get the red carpet treatment, especially since it was Ms. Sprewell that was responsible for his departure from Houston.

"Michael, we also have a proposed offer for writing on Busy Bee's project." Sprewell dialed her assistant's extension while twirling a pen in the opposite hand. "Um, Amanda please bring the file labeled Michael Fletcher."

Mr. Johnson leaned forward and clapped his hands. "Michael, we will meet with Busy Bee this evening at dinner. He absolutely loves your tracks and is very excited to start working on the project."

As the two gentlemen conversed, Amanda delivered the file. Ms. Sprewell handed the file to him as she spoke, "Michael, we want to give you time to review your offer and reconvene in a couple of hours to address any concerns you may have. In the meantime, Amanda will escort you to your office."

As they walked out, he took a glance at the offer sheet. He looked for specific things, such as a base pay and a satisfactory unit rate for mechanical and performance royalties. His eyes quickly scanned for the bottom line figures. He failed to locate the numbers because he was preoccupied with where Amanda would lead him. Once again, he walked through Greece hoping he had a small villa nestled somewhere in the theater district. He expected her to walk toward the elevators. Instead, she made a right and a quick left aiming for the corner office that perfectly lined up with an elevated paparazzi view of the Staples Center.

"Oh this is sweet! Look at this view!"

Amanda smiled as she readjusted her eyeglasses. "We thought you would be impressed. If you think this is something, wait until the sun goes down and the Staples Center is lit up."

Michael was left alone to soak it all in. Before taking pictures and sending them to Jasmine, he felt he should sit down and go through the file. Once he settled in, he felt it was a lucrative offer with only one discrepancy. He figured it wouldn't be a huge wrinkle to iron out when they reconvened. Fletch leaned back into his executive chair and placed his feet on his mahogany-finished desk as he took pictures with his phone. "My crew will not believe this!" After taking a few shots, Fletch sent them to Jasmine and the boys. He was thankful for them supporting his decision to come to Los Angeles. He planned to bring them up once the project was rolling and he got familiar with the city. When he sat down with Sprewell later that afternoon, he expressed his gratitude for such a plush office and addressed the one glitch in his offer sheet. Michael noticed the contract didn't include any synchronization royalties. That ensured he would receive payment for any of Busy Bee's music used in movies, television shows, and commercials. Ms. Sprewell seemed surprised that detail was omitted. She apologized for the oversight and assured him it would be added and ready for his signature by the end of the week. Michael appreciated her genuineness and promptness to address his concern. He thought, "Maybe she won't be too bad after all."

Days turned into weeks and Michael was settling into the Cali lifestyle. He worked countless hours on the project. Artists are notorious for working Dracula-like hours; therefore, going in and out of the studio and spending uncomfortable nights on the couch in his office was a common occurrence. Things were moving along smoothly and Tracy Sprewell liked Michael's aggressive work ethics. Before long, she started attending Busy's recording sessions as a representative of corporate management. Sprewell attempted to maintain her professionalism during the sessions. However, there were times she was found slightly moving her curvaceous body to the beat of Michael's tracks while privately lip-syncing the lyrics he wrote. Everyone wondered why she was showing up at the after-hours sessions like a groupie masquerading as an exec. Michael didn't pay any attention to her presence other than the boss was being visible. Of course, Busy thought she wanted a younger man and she was feeling his persona as an artist and sex symbol.

Brandon Stephens a.k.a. Busy Bee was a gifted seventeen-year-old rapper who showed maturity beyond his years. He wasn't the stereotypical young man who decided to throw all his eggs in one basket and become a rapper. Stephens was multitalented. When talking with him, you instantly recognized his educated responses, as well as noticing his leadership skills. Furthermore, he drew Michael's attention when it was publicized that he refused to use profanity in his music. That alone indicated he was a cut above the norm, especially when you consider the blatant disrespect many kids his age display daily in their respective schools and social environments. Believe it or not, many hip-hop blogs and publications had negative things to say about his decision to keep his music clean. Many underground artists and fans felt his music would be cheesy and didn't have a chance to survive on the streets. People wanted catchy hooks and hard-core lyrics that created images to vicariously live through. It was written any label that signed Busy had money to burn. Surprisingly, the negative talk came to a screeching halt, once he released his first single. Retracted statements were popping up all over the web like buttered popcorn! All of a sudden, his style was what the industry needed to curve the negative perception of rap music. Rap magazines referred to him as, "The New Sensation!" His ability to make people listen to what he had to say was in his smooth delivery and God-given cadence on the microphone. Once he had your attention, the metaphors that hammered home his message in his music left listeners replaying his song over and over. Any clueless college marketing major could recognize the potential marketing dollars with an artist like Busy. He was asked during an interview, "Who thought of the concept to keep the music clean?"

He responded, "Well, to be honest I got the idea after reading 'The Road Not Taken' by Robert Frost. I decided to find ways to speak without trying to sound or act like any other artist. At the end of the day, daring to be different in a positive way could potentially have a positive change on our culture."

Brandon was very educated and displayed a knack to work very hard at everything he touched. Therefore, it wasn't much of a surprise that he was in the top fifteen percent of his class and vowed to break the top ten percent before his high school days concluded. In addition, he was an extraordinary high school basketball player. Many Division I universities were recruiting him to add to their backcourt. He stood six feet and played like he was six feet five inches. Clearly, he was special and handsome to boot. However, he was completely off track thinking Ms.

Sprewell would fall for the young up and coming star and relinquish her seat at the roundtable of music executives that crushed and granted dreams to aspiring musicians like the U.S. Supreme Court.

Periodically, Mr. Johnson had to ask the engineer to cut the music and have Busy refocus and stop gawking at Tracy. She seemed to have a mind-altering effect on the youngster whenever she entered the room. Mr. Johnson whispered to Michael in a jokingly way, "Man, Sprewell has the young fella stuttering instead of rapping."

Michael laughed and replied, "Yeah, he looks like a young Adam being mesmerized by Eve!"

Johnson added, "I'm not going to lie. Sprewell would have had all the disciples saying, 'Jesus, you go ahead. We'll catch up with you later!'"

Michael laughed once again and shook his head. "Johnson, boy, you're going to hell for that one."

Chapter 6

. . . Adjusting to Distance

B ack in Houston, the Fletcher family missed their captain. Time passed and Jasmine struggled to fill the empty space Michael occupied in her life. Although the boys missed the big guy as well, they seemed to adjust a little better than their mom. They didn't show obvious signs of despair. In fact, they spent much of their social time bragging to their friends about their dad doing it big in Los Angeles. After several late nights with the case of the crying spells, Jasmine purposed in her heart to be content with working, taking care of the kids, and long conversations with her husband on the phone or video chatting when possible. Eventually, she would take a trip to California, but for the time being, Marvin Gaye's love ballad, *Distant Lover,* was the appropriate song for their relationship. Jason and Cynthia were on the fast track to getting their own place. They decided on an apartment ten minutes away. Knowing they would be in close proximity seemed to console Jasmine.

In desperate need of some girl time, Jasmine had Paige over for dinner. "Girl, I am so glad you called and invited me over, although I will admit I almost canceled. I had a very handsome man ask me out for drinks. I almost slid into my drool dress and took a rain check for our evening."

Jasmine looked somewhat confused. "Wait a minute. What is a drool dress?"

Paige stood up and walked to the fireplace like a runway model as she responded. "Girl, that's a dress that guarantees any man to drool like a breastfed baby when I strut in front of him!"

They both screamed in laughter as Paige fell on the couch. "Jasmine, we need to go out and listen to some music. I think you'll enjoy getting out and unwinding."

Mrs. Fletcher sipped on her glass of Moscato, as she sat Indian style on the love seat. "Paige, I don't know about that. I haven't been out in so long; I would probably fall asleep at the table. Plus, I don't want all those men in my face thinking two drinks will get them in the door."

Paige shook her head in humorous pity. "Aw, it has been a while for you. I see we will have to whip you into shape. When my girlfriends and I go out, we collectively run guys like that away like wounded dogs. Trust me. The likelihood of a loser penetrating our walls of protection is slim to none. I have a trained tactical diva squad that has taken down the best of them."

They laughed once again, and for the first time since Michael's departure, Jasmine considered going out and having a little fun. "OK, maybe it would be good to get out and enjoy myself." They agreed to go out the following weekend. Their night peacefully ended with chocolate, popcorn, and a Tyler Perry movie.

The following week went by like a rushing wind and Jasmine found herself sitting in her office that Friday afternoon contemplating on pulling out of the festivities Paige planned for her and her group of divas. She thought of several excuses that she could present to Paige. However, she imagined Paige dispelling each one with a well-supported argument to win her case. All of a sudden, she abandoned the book of excuses. She seemed to snap out of her negative trance when she thought of Michael's unavailability for the last four days. "Wait, why am I denying myself? I need to get out of that house before I crack up. Besides, I'm sure Fletch is living it up on the west coast." She tried not to think negatively when they didn't speak to each other. She simply chalked it up to the woes of a long-distance relationship. However, today, she needed the woes to motivate her to step out with the girls for some fun. Obviously, it worked because she called Paige soon after reaching her decision. "Hey, girl! What's the plan for tonight?"

Paige responded in a somewhat bewildered voice. "Hello, hello, who is this? I know this isn't Jasmine because I pictured her thinking of ways to cancel her plans to hang with me."

Jasmine laughed, "Girl, you know me too well. However, tonight I am ready to have a good time. I may not wear a drool dress, but when Jasmine Fletcher walk in the place, the music will stop."

"OK, I hear you talking like a diva! I want you to know I did take the liberty to create a sign that reads, 'I'm married,' in efforts to discourage the guys that make it a point to ignore a woman's ring finger. It's a cute sign that actually covers your puppies. I think you'll like it."

They both got a kick out of Paige's sarcasm. "Um, no I won't need any signs. Trust me. I know how to handle the smooth talkers."

Jasmine didn't have any problems turning men away. She neglected to tell Michael of the countless invites to strolls in the park, theatrical plays, and dinner while working at Stevenson Engineering. Fletch wouldn't have seen the humor in his wife being asked to drinks during happy hour at a fancy hotel where the guy ironically had a key to a room. Jasmine knew the game guys played better than she led people to believe. As she drove home, she began to prioritize her evening. The first task was to ask Jason and Cynn to make sure the boys were squared away with dinner. Next, scan her wardrobe to find an after-five selection that's sexy, yet classy. If there ever were a woman that aged beautifully, it would be Mrs. Fletcher. She looked ten years younger than her actual age. Although her demeanor could be viewed as tranquil, she expected men to approach her when she was in social surroundings. Secretly, she enjoyed having the power to grant or deny access into her world. Admittedly, Fletch was the only man that had ever penetrated her walls of dominance and rendered her helpless and subservient to love and lust. As she pulled in front of their home, Jason and his nephews were hanging out in the garage clowning around as he changed a defective brake light on his car.

"Well, hello, guys! What's the topic today?"

Brandon looked at his mom and responded, "Not today, Mom. The talk today is strictly for the fellas."

Jasmine produced a devilish grin. "Jason, what are you telling my boys about girls? I know you. Chris is too young to walk around here thinking he's a sex symbol."

Chris placed his hand on Jasmine's shoulder in consolation. "Mom, I don't know how to break it to ya, but I accepted that crown in the fifth grade right after the school play when I had the lead role as Daddy Warbucks in *Annie*. The girls loved me after my performance!"

Jason fastened the last screw on the light's casing and added, "I'm not surprised, Chris. That's when it starts. Back in the day, that would have been the dream role for a young stud like me."

Everyone laughed and exchanged high fives except for Jasmine.

"Chris, I thought you only loved your momma."

He reached out to Jasmine and grabbed her hand. "Mom, you are the only woman I love! I'm not in love with any girls yet! Uncle Jason is just teaching me how to select the right girls to place on my team."

Brandon chimed in, "Yeah, Mom, you see from there we choose a starting five and the season begins. Based on their performance, we'll select an MVG. That stands for the most valuable girl. That selection would clearly suggest she might be the one! Am I right, Uncle Jason?"

Jason leaned against the car, shook his head, and clapped in a congratulatory manner as if his pupils were walking the stage to receive their degree. "Yes, you are correct, my brilliant one!"

Being quick-witted, Jasmine fired back. "All I know is you'd better deprogram your students before Rev. Fletch finds out his boys has gone rogue and become Houston's version of Hugh Hefner."

Jasmine was so wrapped into clowning with the guys; she almost forgot to ask Jason to watch the boys while she hit the town.

"Oh, it nearly slipped my mind. Jason, do you and Cynn have any plans tonight?"

Jason thought for a second. "No, not really. We may go and get a bite and take in a movie. Why, what's up?"

"I was wondering if you guys could look after the boys. I made plans to hang with the girls tonight."

Jason walked over to his sister and put his arm around her as they turned to walk into the house.

"Of course, anything for my beautiful sister. You deserve some time to unwind and enjoy yourself. We'll be fine!"

With that taken care of, Jasmine could focus on the evening ahead. After a relaxing bath, she sat in her favorite chair near the bay windows in their bedroom and began polishing her toenails. Minutes later, her cell phone began to play Michael's assigned ringtone. She thought to herself, "Oh, now he wants to call." When she answered, she was greeted with a happy and energetic introduction.

"Well, hello there. How are you?"

Jasmine responded, "I'm doing great! So nice of you to call."

Michael detected a tad bit of sarcasm in her response. However, he continued to be upbeat. "Can you join me on the video chat app before the next recording session begins?"

Jasmine agreed, and when she saw his handsome face, she couldn't continue to be upset with him. "It's nice to hear your voice after four days, Michael."

"I apologize, babe. We've been working at a feverish pitch and I've been under a little pressure. It won't happen again."

They went on to talk for another thirty minutes about the project, the kids, and their desire to see each other. Before long, it was time for Michael to leave the confines of his office and return to the studio. They both blew a kiss to the screen and proceeded to log out. However, Michael didn't log out properly. It was normal for Jasmine to wait until Michael was completely gone because she never liked to disconnect first. While she waited, she heard a knock on Michael's office door and a woman's voice entering the room. Jasmine had no idea who the woman was. When Tracy Sprewell appeared in the screen, Jasmine's heart began to beat a little faster. Instantly, she noticed the sophisticated beauty Sprewell elegantly flaunted. Sprewell took a seat and began to talk to Michael.

"Come on slow poke. I knew you wouldn't be ready."

Michael was unaware his wife was tuning in. "I'm almost ready. I had to tie up some loose ends."

Sprewell crossed her legs and replied in an authoritative, yet seductive manner, "I see. So I assume there won't be any interruptions tonight."

Michael walked toward Tracy and stood in front of the screen. Although Jasmine could still hear, her view was very limited.

"Yes, ma'am, we should get through the night without any interruptions from my end."

Jasmine began to fill with anger. Primarily, because he referred to talking to her as tying a loose end. She thought, "Was calling me his attempt to clear his to-do-list to be with that woman?" She wasn't sure if they were talking about work or something more private. She wanted to know why Michael's tone changed. Before she could yell out Michael's name, her screen went blank. She hurried to reach Michael on his cell phone. Unfortunately, the next six calls went directly to his voice mail. Needless to say, Jasmine found herself in a panicked state of mind. She thought, "How could he do this to me?" As she paced the perimeter of their walk-in closet, her cell phone began to play Michael's ringtone once again. Jasmine answered aggressively, "Michael, you are a sorry excuse of a man! I can't believe what I just saw!"

Fletcher's head began to swim with confusion. "Whoa, whoa, wait a minute! What are you talking about? I just called you back because I saw all the missed calls."

"Who is she Michael? Who is the woman that came into your office and had you talking low and seductive? Yes, I saw it all from your screen when you thought you disconnected from me!"

Once he understood why Jasmine was in an uproar, his heart rate began to decrease.

"Sweetheart, that was my boss! Furthermore, my tone didn't change into anything. I was being professional, not seductive. She asked me if I was ready to go to the studio and start our session with Busy. What did you think I was doing?"

Jasmine knew what she heard. Michael's explanation was falling on deaf ears. "Michael, go with your boss and do whatever you were on your way to do. I'm fine. That definitely explains why we haven't talked in days!" Jasmine hung up in his face and threw the phone on the bed. She refused to consider Michael's version of what happened. She sat on the edge of her bed and replayed the event in her mind. She thought, "Maybe he was telling the truth. Michael is a good guy. However, that woman was amazingly beautiful! I can't be that naive to think he wouldn't consider flirting with her. All men cheat at some point. Why should I sit here and be a victim?"

Jasmine always had the ability to refocus and do what she felt was best for her. After processing everything, she planned to go out and not let Michael ruin her evening. As she stood in the closet, she continued to vent. "I should wear a drool dress tonight! I can't believe he allowed that woman to be so casual with him. Huh, he was only being professional. Doesn't that fool realize I know him better than he knows himself? How idiotic is it for him to think I didn't recognize the same tone he's used with me whenever he was trying to be sexy! I need a drink!"

Meanwhile, Michael struggled to focus on his work, he was worried about what happened. He knew there was nothing going on with Tracy and trying to explain that kind of stuff to a distant love was extremely difficult.

It was apparent Michael wasn't himself. Tracy picked up on his frustrations and offered a quick fix. "Michael, where's your mind right now? How about we have Busy go through some of his recorded songs and complete the retakes we talked about? Johnson and I will treat you to a few drinks to take the edge off."

Michael didn't know if that was a good idea considering she was the topic of his frustration. However, he knew he wouldn't be productive in his present state of mind. Therefore, he agreed to walk a couple of blocks down the street to Marcel Lounge.

Marcel Lounge was a hangout for the affluent that was setup on prime real estate. Ms. Sprewell informed Johnson, Busy Bee, and the engineer of their plans. Johnson responded, "If we're going to do the retakes, I would like to stay and give some input." Tracy didn't mind Johnson staying, considering her main focus was to clear Michael's head. She agreed and turned toward Fletch. "Are you ready?"

Michael nodded his head and stood up. Tracy took lead and headed toward the door while he noticed Johnson remained seated and engaged in conversation with the engineer. "Johnson, let's go, man."

Johnson turned around and replied, "Oh, I'm not going chief. I told Tracy I wanted to stay while Busy go through the retakes."

Fletch began to wonder if this was a setup. "Is Tracy up to something? Did Jasmine observe something I missed? Did I sound seductive in my office?" The last thing Michael wanted was Jasmine to feel he was cheating on her. A slew of *what ifs* raced through his mind. What if he miscalculated and discovered Tracy was only being a concerned supervisor? On the other hand, what if Sprewell was indeed interested and was trying to lure him like an animal in heat? What if this emergency excursion to the lounge was the beginning of a steamy affair? Most importantly, what about Jasmine? Michael continued to walk with Tracy while fearing the worse. In addition, he found it very hard to stay focused on God's way of doing things as he watched the swaying of her hypnotic hips. Fletcher never cheated on his wife, and it seemed his resolve to continue as a faithful man was being challenged. He never crossed the line with

Tracy; however, Jasmine's accusations created suspicion. Once they walked into Marcel's, Michael sort of snapped back to himself. He looked around the room and couples were engaged in conversations, while the one-line pickup artists were running through their gigolo material with every lady at the bar. He thought, "What am I doing here? I should be back at the studio working."

Sprewell found two spots at the bar. "So how about we have a couple of drinks and see if you can relax and let your creativity take over?"

After speaking, she crossed her legs displaying her thighs as she got the attention of the bartender. Michael mentally salivated as he marveled at the smooth texture of her skin and muscular detail of her quads and hamstrings. Things were not looking good for his marriage.

Tracy continued, "What would you like, Michael?"

He refocused, "Um, I'll have a Tequila Sunrise."

She tapped him on the knee, while ordering. "OK, that sounds good! We'll have two please. Michael if you don't mind me asking, what's wrong with you? It's obvious you're not yourself."

He wanted to tell her the absolute truth, but better judgment prevailed. "Well, let's just say marriage is work; and sometimes, it's harder when you are apart."

Sprewell looked on with a sincere look of concern and replied, "OK, I knew it had to be something meaningful to throw you off, because when you are working, you're like a machine. I understand it's hard on you and your family. I do appreciate your diligence to complete this project."

"We were actually talking about taking a couple of weeks off due to Brandon's schedule with school and college visits for basketball."

"How about we pay for your family to fly up and spend some much-needed time with you. We can send you in a limo and meet them. We are very pleased with your work and want to help in any way. On a personal note, I like the way you carry yourself. I may need to introduce you to my fiancée and let you take him under your wing and give him a few pointers on being a good husband. I'm the type when I stand before a minister and say I do, I don't plan to stand before a judge five years later and say I don't."

As she finished talking, someone shouted across the room, "Pete, over here!" Once he processed what Tracy said and heard the name Pete, Michael's spiritual tank began to fill with a God conscious. The bartender was making his way over with their order. Michael said, "You know, maybe we don't need the drinks. I should probably order a soda instead."

Tracy smiled, "Good call. Sir, I'm sorry, but can we change that to sodas?"

The bartender responded, "No problem, two sodas coming right up!"

The fear of things getting out of hand boiled down to a very low simmer. Michael began to relax a little as he spoke, "I don't know what to say. I'm glad you all see my dedication to the project. And yes, seeing my family will make me very happy. They're going to be ecstatic about coming out to California! Now, enough about me. What's the deal with a marriage on the horizon? When am I going to meet him?"

Tracy began to light up with the opportunity to talk about her future husband. "Well, his name is Darian Webster and we've been dating for four years. He's a pharmacist here in Los Angeles. He has a beautiful personality and is a very handsome guy. I love to see him in that sexy white lab coat! He treats me like a queen and I enjoy reciprocating his love. We are planning on getting married next year." Michael smiled and added, "And there it is!" Tracy looked a bit confused and looked around, "There what is?" Michael laughed. "There's the reason the project was rerouted to Los Angeles. Somebody didn't want to leave their man." Tracy leaned back in laughter, "No. See, you got it all wrong. I didn't do that. That decision was made by the big wigs. Now, don't get me wrong, I was definitely in favor of the decision. No other woman was going to be wearing my man's lab coat and making breakfast for him while I'm riding horses in Texas with you guys." Michael responded, "Oh, you got jokes!"

As Tracy spoke of Darian, Michael couldn't help but to think of Alexis. He was taken back to the kitchen table of his parents' home and the drive from the police station with Alexis after Ray's death. He knew energetic optimistic love when he heard it. He began to see Sprewell as he saw Alexis. It was like he was spending time with his other younger sister from the west coast. He realized once again God had taken a potential lustful situation and used it for his glory. They talked for another hour as Michael shared some spiritual things with her. As they walked out of the lounge, they had the look of siblings as opposed to colleagues. Michael returned to the studio with renewed energy to work. Johnson looked at Michael and said, "Are you drunk? Ya'll both walked in laughing and smiling like you had several rounds."

Michael laughed, "Johnson if you can get drunk off of soda, I'm loaded!"

Tracy laughed, "Yeah, we just had sodas and talked. So what have you guys been able to accomplish?"

Back in Houston, Jasmine was pulling up in front of the nightclub. The valet walked over and handed her a ticket as she called Paige's phone to announce her arrival. Unbeknownst to Jasmine, Paige and her SUV of divas pulled to the valet stand behind her. Seeing the girls and their smiles took Jasmine's mind off of Michael. Excitement was in the air as four stunning ladies fit for the red carpet exited the black Cadillac Escalade. Paige instantly noticed Jasmine and screamed, "Girl, what are you doing in that drool dress? You know you don't want that kind of attention tonight!"

Her dress hugged her curves and revealed enough of her legs to draw attention from seventy five percent of the men in the club. Her makeup was flawless, compliments of Cynthia and her many talents. To be honest, Jasmine looked like a slightly older version of Tracy Sprewell.

"Tonight, it's about me and the ladies. I will not spend time thinking about Michael. You have my word on that!"

Paige looked her up and down and replied, "OK, I don't know what happened to you, but I like it!"

In a celebratory fashion, she shouted, "Ladies, shall we?" They all walked in a synchronized strut as the bouncer held the door open for them. Before they could reach for their purses, the club manager dressed in a nicely fitted suit politely stopped the ladies from producing forms of payment and offered the VIP section as a courtesy. Paige accepted and soon thereafter, the divas were escorted to their manicured nest. Jasmine liked the attention as she paced her walk to notice men paying homage to their self-proclaimed royalty. The night was young; the music was blaring. It was definitely a party atmosphere. If you were a single lady, there was a very good stock of men to choose from. The ages ranged from twenty-eight to forty-five. Club Elegance seemed to draw many professional walks of life. The disc jockey showed his ability to control the atmosphere by playing songs that kept a consistent crowd on the dance floor. No matter what genre of music he chose, it seemed to ignite a united roar of approval at the beginning of each song. It's a proven theory that as long as the music is hot and people are dancing, the bar is making money. Buying and selling drinks were being negotiated like trading on Wall Street. Jasmine seemed to settle into the social atmosphere without looking like an overwhelmed married woman. However, inside, she tucked away some steam for Michael. Although she purposed in her heart to enjoy herself, it wasn't totally motivated by the desire to let her hair down. She was upset with Michael and this was a way of leveling the playing field.

Before long, the waitress brought a complimentary setup of drinks for the ladies. Paige and the girls didn't know why they were being treated so nicely, but they didn't dare question it. After a few drinks, Jasmine transferred her feelings from Michael and legitimately began to have fun. Guys were in and out of their section like planes arriving and departing from theairport. A couple of pilots were successful in securing a sexy dance partner while they sent majority of the airmen away with rejected faces. As the music blasted through the speakers, Paige leaned over to shout in Jasmine's ear. "Girl, do you see the guy in the white shirt with his back to the bar?" Jasmine played it off and glanced like she was just surveying the area.

"You mean the one with his arms folded looking like Boris Kodjoe? 'Cause he is fine! Oh my goodness!"

Paige took a sip of her drink, nodded, and rushed to respond. "Yes! He has been staring at you for the last ten minutes! If he makes a move, remember you can't! I am going to guide his plane onto my landing strip!" The two of them leaned back in laughter while holding hands in agreement.

After Paige brought it to her attention, she noticed him gazing at her and she felt a girlish excitement shoot through her body. Her spirit tried to fight the temptations of the flesh. The more she clandestinely glanced at the bar, the weaker she became. Her spiritual resolve began to fade as she failed to ignore his silent advance. When Jasmine began to take a scheduled panoramic scan to where he was standing, she shockingly discovered he had abandoned his post and was headed directly toward her. Her heart began to beat rapidly. She hit Paige's leg to warn her that Air Force One was about to land. Without a shadow of a doubt, Jasmine nominated the Kodjoe look-alike for president of Club Elegance! Paige was certain Jasmine wouldn't entertain his advances. Therefore, she straightened her clothes and sat with the capture pose. With an arch in her back, she turned to her left side, crossed her legs, and made sure her derriere and toned thighs were a major focal point. As he got closer, Jasmine began to give way to the possibility of getting to know this mystery pilot. She also struck a sexy pose while placing both hands on her right knee.

"Hello, ladies, may I join you?"

Aspiring divas would notice Paige's ability to be cool in the saddle. She was a pro at hiding her hormonal jumping jellybeans. She flirtatiously responded, "Sure, you're welcome to sit with us if you can handle being with real women. Our VIP status is a daily thing."

Jasmine gave Paige a look that said, "Girl, I like that!"

111

"I'm sure I'll be able to last a little longer than the last six guys that you devoured. By the way, my name is Adrian Moore."

Surprisingly, Jasmine beat Paige's extension and offered her hand for the customary shake. However, appearing to be a romantic throwback, he gently grabbed her hand and lightly kissed her soft skin. His perfectly shaped lips slowly rolled off her hand as he purposely looked into her eyes. It was obvious he wanted Jasmine. While hiding her off hand from Adrian, Paige slithered it along the backside of the sofa like a camouflaged viper and pinched Jasmine. The three of them continued to socialize, while the other divas conducted a few meet and greets. Despite her marital status, Jasmine found Adrian intriguing. She couldn't help but wonder how lucky any woman would be to have this man's arms encompassing their body. Jasmine allowed her mind to escape her life with Michael and imagined Adrian's body next to hers. She was definitely living in the moment. Paige noticed how freely Jasmine opened up to Adrian during their private question and answer segment. She sensed something had triggered this behavior, so she took the liberty to pencil Jasmine in for an extensive inquiry at a later date.

The night ended with Adrian walking out of the club with the ladies. Paige's vehicle arrived from valet and she apprehensively walked toward the driver's side. She didn't want to leave Jasmine alone with Adrian fearing she would see a new sunrise from an unfamiliar room with a man she just met.

Paige shouted from inside of her vehicle, "Jasmine, I'm going to pull over and wait until your car arrives! We come together, we leave together."

Adrian was an intelligent guy. He knew that was code talk for, "Don't even think about it." He turned to Jasmine and looked her in the eyes, "Well, I guess that's my cue to call it an evening. It was a pleasure meeting you. From what I know about you thus far, you are an amazing woman."

Before he could turn away, Jasmine grabbed his hand. Paige and the girls observed from a perfectly placed parking spot to witness the closing statements and were shocked when they saw Jasmine reach out to grab Adrian.

"It was a pleasure to meet you as well. I was wondering if we could keep in touch. I mean, I think you would make a great friend." They agreed to exchange numbers. Shortly thereafter, her car arrived and everyone headed home. During the ride home, Jasmine didn't feel she crossed the line with Adrian. Once she was physically removed from Club Elegance, thoughts of Michael began to resurface. This time, she didn't feel as angry. She thought to herself, "Well, if he has a working relationship with an attractive woman, I shouldn't feel guilty establishing a friendship with an attractive man."

Due to the routine of life, Jasmine and Paige went three weeks before they had a chance to sit and spill the tea. Paige scheduled a lunch date with Jasmine in order to begin her inquisition.

They decided to meet at a nice bistro in the downtown area that had a lovely backdrop of Houston's theater district and water features that provided a much-needed getaway of the hustle and bustle of corporate America. Paige arrived ahead of schedule to gain possession of the table on the patio that sat center stage. Before long, Jasmine walked over and pulled out her seat as she greeted Paige. "Well, hello, lady! I see you worked your magic once again and got the best seats in the house!"

Paige laughed, "Yeah, you know me. How are you today?"

Jasmine sat down and replied, "I'm good. I have another big project going on and it's getting on my nerves. So if you see my hair falling out, you'll know why."

"Well anyway, you know I have a million questions to ask you. I plan to get all in your business today!"

Jasmine laughed, "Trust me, I came expecting you to drill me like a detective. I just didn't know how long you were going to dance around the elephant in the room."

"Oh, you mean that elephant named Adrian?"

Jasmine smiled, "Yeah, that one."

"So I assume you've talked to him since the night at the club. I am going to be honest. I thought you were just a little tipsy and by morning you would had snapped back into yourself again."

"You're right. I was a little tipsy. However, we've talked maybe once or twice since then, but it was just small talk. There is no reason for you to be alarmed."

Paige listened to Jasmine and knew it was virtually impossible to be platonic friends with a man like Adrian. It was open season to ask about Adrian, but she felt a little hesitant to ask about Michael. She understood her boundaries as a friend and tried her best to ease into a question about him.

"Sweetie, there's something I was wondering and I wanted to ask, but I fear you will take offense to me asking."

Jasmine answered, "No, ask what you like. There is only one thing I will never discuss and that's my sex life with my man!" They both laughed. "But seriously, ask and I'll tell you if I don't want to answer."

Paige's voice transitioned into a sincere, caring voice as she inquired, "I watched you the other night and the lady I saw was not the lady that I envisioned prior to meeting up. It was like you were trying to prove something. I didn't know if you were making sure you fit in or what. I'm just wondering if everything is OK with you and Michael. I don't want to pry into your marriage, but if you need to talk, I'm here."

Jasmine listened and processed what Paige was saying. She really didn't want to talk to her about it, but she feared she would eventually.

"Well, I'll admit that night I was upset with Michael about some things. Now that I'm a few weeks removed from it, I realize it may or may not have been that big of a deal. I overheard a conversation between him and his female boss discussing the project he's working on after he thought he disconnected from our video chat. I guess it bothered me because the woman was young and incredibly beautiful!"

Paige kept a straight face while Jasmine explained. When the time came to speak, she carefully asked, "So was that the driving force behind you opening up at the club the other night?

Honestly, Jasmine wasn't totally convinced her actions were out of anger. Her attraction to Adrian took her off guard. He challenged her judgmental views in regard to unfaithful women. Mr. Moore was a potential problem, but she wasn't going to tell Paige that, just like she wasn't going to tell Paige the truth about how many times she talked to Adrian. She actually communicated with him many times since the night at the club. She knew she loved Michael, but Adrian somehow tapped into a side of her that remained dormant deep inside. Without the temptation of another man, Jasmine didn't realize how being a wife, a mom, and career woman created a creature of habit within her. Although she loved her family and their life, she flirted with the idea of spontaneity. Needless to say, Adrian's presence challenged her comfortable lifestyle. He seemed to be the guy that could enable her to experience things without obligation. He was different from Michael in that aspect. Perhaps, she never stopped to think it was because he didn't have the responsibility Michael shouldered as her husband. Nevertheless, Adrian quickly got into her psyche, and Jasmine didn't want to analyze how he got there. She secretly hid the excitement of his presence and convinced herself as long as he is titled *friend*, she wouldn't be in violation of infidelity. Therefore, as she sat with Paige, she chose not to reveal her true feelings. Paige loved having fun, but she was a godly woman at the end of the day. Jasmine knew if she told the truth, Paige would say something to trigger her thinking that would lead her away from Adrian. Instead, she gave an insipid answer that would be easy for Paige to digest. Jasmine continued to answer Paige's question about Michael, "Yes, I was upset with him and figured I deserved to have a good time. At first, I thought about pulling out of going, but my anger would have escalated if I just sat there. Getting out helped me release some steam. When we met Adrian, it was just a way of getting back at Michael. Don't worry, girl, I'm back to the old me."

Paige added, "Well, I'm glad you're back. We both know all Satan need is a small mix up to create a huge mess up! So has he contacted you since?"

Jasmine replied, "Who, Michael?"

Paige answered, "Yes, girl. Your husband!"

"Of course, I've talked to him and we're good."

Paige switched from Michael to Adrian, "So what was Adrian talking about when you two talked?"

Jasmine returned, "When he called I didn't get a chance to answer, so he left a voice mail. I did return his call and we just chatted for a bit about work and things like that. It wasn't anything earth-shaking. The conversation stayed on the surface."

"OK, that's innocent enough. Be careful, Jasmine. You can't talk to him every day and expect not to be tempted to go out with him. It is very difficult to not want a man like that around."

Jasmine desperately wanted to change the subject because she was lying about the phone calls and the way she viewed Adrian. Paige had no idea how precise she was when she said it's difficult to not want him around. As the lunch date proceeded, Jasmine found a way to derail that conversation. They began talking about a stage play they wanted to see, among other girly things. Jasmine didn't consider what was happening during her time with Paige. For the first time in her marriage, she didn't want to hear sound advice that would protect or strengthen her union with Michael. Her curious flesh encouraged her to deflect Paige's advances to clear her head of any misguided intentions.

Chapter 7

...From Drizzle to Rain

D ays passed and another Saturday morning had arrived. Jasmine decided to sleep in a little later than usual. Jason, Brandon, and Chris were already gone to the gym for an early workout. Cynthia had a workshop to attend; therefore, she had the entire house to herself. As the sun penetrated the custom-made curtains in their master suite, Jasmine laid with her eyes fixated on the glow of light God freely provided for her. Many things crossed her mind as she listened to the creatures of the air chirp an original good morning song. Her thoughts wrapped around the fact the she missed her husband. Being reduced to talking to him on the phone was taking a toll on her. While longing for his morning touch, Satan fought desperately to replace her thoughts of Michael's absence with the availability of Adrian's friendship. The mental and emotional battle occupied her morning. She knew in her heart the argument she had with

Michael wasn't that big of a deal. As she positioned herself in a fetal position, she began to feel guilty about letting Adrian into her world. He didn't earn the right to be there. Every marriage goes through its challenges and the Fletchers had their share over the years. She began to put her flesh under the microscope to see the ugliness she was allowing in when her purse began to vibrate. She stretched to the other side of the bed to grab her designer bag to do a customary search and recover through an array of female essentials. Her hands scrambled through important stuff like shopping receipts, a billfold, a tube of lipstick, perfume, keys, lotion, a bottle of ibuprofen, and the gold mine of loose change that covered the floor of her oversized backpack. After that maneuver, she finally grabbed and answered the phone without looking at the number on the screen. To her surprise, she was greeted with a second song of the morning. This time, it was a human voice, a sexy, talented voice. Jasmine initially thought Michael had a recording artist call with a singing telegram to creatively introduce their day of long-distance love. However, at the end of the serenade, she discovered it was actually Adrian that emitted the Brian McKnight–type sounds through the phone. Although thoughts of Michael dominated her mind prior to her phone ringing, Jasmine seemed to switch gears like a race car driver to respond to Adrian's creative greeting.

"Adrian, what in the world? I didn't know you had such a beautiful voice! Oh my goodness, you sounded like a professional."

Adrian replied, "I thought that would wake you up. How are you this morning?"

She answered, "I'm doing OK. I'm still in the bed. Today is one of those days."

"I understand. You're a hardworking woman. You deserve to have a day of relaxation. Did you have any plans other than resting?"

Jasmine responded, "Well, other than picking up a few things from the grocery store, my day is free. My kids are with my brother and I have the house to myself."

"Sounds like you are happy about having some me time. I guess I can't compete with that."

Jasmine asked, "What do you mean compete?"

"Well, I wanted to invite you to an event at the Fine Arts Museum of Houston this afternoon. A very close friend of mine has a collection that's being featured. Each year, the museum chooses a local artist to feature during an event called the *Discovery Series*. It's a great opportunity for aspiring artists to get their work out there. Collectors and fine arts officials from all over come out and share in the event. The goal is to have your work displayed in other art museums around the country or actually have it purchased by collectors. It's really a big deal."

"Wow, I know your friend is excited. I wouldn't mind going, but I don't know if that's a wise choice."

Adrian pleaded, "Come on, it's just a chance to hang out as friends. I promise I will be a complete gentleman and respect your situation."

Jasmine questioned, "My situation?"

"Well, I meant to say your marriage."

"I don't know, Adrian. Let me think about that. What time does it start?"

He returned, "It begins at four o'clock. If you choose to join me, call me by two. If not, I'll definitely understand."

As Jasmine said goodbye, her mind began to race. "I wouldn't mind going, but can I handle being around him? Yes, yes I can. Just be his friend and have an innocent day of fun." Jasmine continued to justify her decision to meet Adrian. "It would be different from what I'm used to. I might find an interest in the arts."

She never admitted to herself that Adrian was the focal point. She didn't see Satan's plan to have her compromise her marriage. His moves to confuse her were subtle, yet precise.

Satan knew Jasmine wasn't a bitter wife who had been hurt by her husband through infidelity and neglect. She wasn't a scorned woman looking to restore her self-esteem and independence. She didn't need a leaning post in the form of another man to provide extrinsic motivation to move beyond a failing marriage. She loved her husband. However, she was foolish to think that alone would prevent her from falling. Metaphorically speaking, a storm was brewing and she didn't pay attention to the weather report. She felt the Adrian situation was merely a light drizzle. It was so light; she considered it a harmless mist to cool off the day.

Once making her decision to meet Adrian, she phoned him and confirmed she would attend the event. Adrian was ecstatic but managed to give a friendlike response. He didn't want Jasmine thinking he had other motives. Before long, they met in front of the museum.

He greeted her with a perfect smile, "Well, I see you made it."

"Yes, how long have you been waiting?"

"Oh, about ten minutes. You look stunning!"

"Thank you! You're not too bad yourself, sir."

After exchanging pleasantries, they entered the building. Upon their entry, a curator introduced himself.

"Hello, Mr. Moore. I'm Tom Webster, the museum's curator. We met when the selection committee went to view Mr. Bourda's collection."

"Good afternoon, Mr. Webster. Now that you've mentioned it, I do recall meeting you. It's a pleasure to see you again. I would like to introduce my good friend Jasmine Fletcher."

Mr. Webster acknowledged Jasmine. "How do you do madam?"

Jasmine replied, "I'm doing great. It's nice to meet you, Mr. Webster."

Adrian looked around as he appreciated the setup. "It seems like you guys did a great job promoting the event. It's quite a few people here already."

"Yes, we are very excited about Mr. Bourda's collection. His work exemplifies our goal for the *Discovery Series*. If you will follow me, he's designated you both as his distinguished guests."

Jasmine was impressed with Adrian's social circle. As she looked around, she seconded Adrian's appreciation for such an elegant event. The artwork was impeccable. Jackson Bourda's work consisted of sculptures, oil paintings, abstract mosaics, and a moving piece of the Resurrection of Jesus. Soft music set the mood, as the pianist's fingers seemed to join hands with the artwork to lure enthusiasts closer to its implied message. Jasmine found herself captivated with one particular piece that was displayed on the back wall of the room. It was a simple, yet moving painting on a huge wall-sized canvas encased by a beautiful hand-carved wooden frame.

It was a picture of a woman on her knees in the middle of an open field. As she looked into the sky, she held a transparent box that seemed to house scenes from her life. The images were very detailed. There were scenes of the birth of her child, a scene of her sitting alone with tears in her eyes, a depiction of her placing flowers on a grave, as well as other highs and lows of her life. Her face was aged, and her grayish hair told of the years she labored in life. Yet she exhibited a glorious smile that caused a ray of light to illuminate her position in the field. In the distance was a man that appeared to be serving as her protection.

As Jasmine listened to the music and escaped into the field, Adrian and Jackson stood behind her as they respectfully allowed her to appreciate the piece. After absorbing the ambiance of the painting, she noticed the presence of the two gentlemen. "Oh, I didn't know you guys were standing there!"

"No problem at all. I just wanted to introduce you to the man of the hour and my childhood buddy, Jackson Bourda. We all call him Jabby."

"Hey, man, don't tell people that! I don't know what's wrong with this guy. It's an honor to meet you Jasmine."

Jasmine replied, "Likewise, Mr. Bourda!"

"Whoa, what's with this Mr. Bourda stuff? Just call me Jackson."

Adrian added, "Or Jabby."

"All right dude. Do you want me to tell some stories about you? I'm sure Jasmine would get a kick out of them. Don't make me downgrade your guest credentials."

When Adrian and Jackson got together, they never managed to be completely mature. They always found time to take shots at each other, all in fun of course.

Jackson probed, "So, Jasmine, obviously, you've found an interest in this painting. I would love to hear your thoughts. What does it say to you?"

Jasmine couldn't wait to share.

"Well, I think this particular piece has a strong spiritual message. As she holds the clear box of her life's experiences, she is saying, 'God, I gladly trust you with my life.' It's like the highs and lows she's experienced never caused her to take her eyes off of God. I think the man in the distance is a representation of the Holy Spirit. I feel it symbolizes the blanket of protection she has over her life."

Jackson and Adrian were impressed with her interpretation. Other enthusiasts began to gather as they listened with enlightened minds while sipping on their glasses of chardonnay. As Jasmine paused to make her next point, an elder in the crowd thought she had concluded her analysis and desperately shouted out, "Please continue!" The congregation concurred, as they wanted more as well. Jasmine was shocked so many had gathered so quickly. Nevertheless, she continued.

"Kneeling in the open field suggests she is showing reverence while surrendering her all. It's saying, through it all cast your cares above with confidence in knowing God will take care of you. Her smile represents her peace within as she's believing God will keep his promise, no matter what she sees around her. With that in mind, I think the message is *there's a comforting peace that comes over your spirit when you decide to trust God with your life.* Oh, one more thing. I think you purposely added extra detail to her smile, the lines in her face, as well as her strands of gray hair. I feel you wanted it to be a focal point as well. It says life will attempt to wear you down. Time will change you, but if you focus on the master, he will provide strength that will put a smile on your face."

When Jasmine finished, the crowd began to clap. Jackson was astounded. Adrian stood with a new admiration for her as he clapped and gave her a look of approval. Mr. Webster walked over to Jackson and whispered in his ear.

"Mr. Bourda, I think this unscheduled critique has been a blessing in disguise. I have just been informed you now have two offers for that painting in the ballpark of 25,000 dollars."

Jackson smiled and before he followed Mr. Webster to meet the potential buyers, he looked at Jasmine and said, "You were great! I have something to share with you in a moment."

Adrian saw a side of Jasmine he'd never encountered in a woman before. He had always been able to corral just about any woman he wanted. Honestly, his charm and physical appearance brought more attention than he would like. Many of the women he dated were beautiful, but few possessed the substance that intrigued him. However, Jasmine presented a challenge. She was an accomplished intellectual. Her beauty was a by-product to the beauty she possessed inside. Adrian felt he needed a woman of her caliber. He briefly imagined what life would be like if she wasn't married.

"Well, you sure know how to command a room."

Jasmine answered, "Thank you, Mr. Moore. I'm glad I was able to enlighten you. I felt so alive! I am so glad you got me out of the house today. I'm having a good time."

Adrian gladly accepted the credit for getting her out. "I'm really happy you're enjoying yourself. I like experiencing moments like this with people I hold dear."

"So are you talking about me or Jabby?"

Adrian grabbed her hand and replied, "Both!"

They began to tour the room slowly as they engaged in a more personal conversation.

"Jasmine, I've noticed you haven't asked me anything like where I live or what I do for a living. That's definitely different from most women I've encountered."

"Well, I'm not most women. Sweetie, I'm what you call one of a kind!"

Adrian gave a sexy grin, "I agree! That's why I like being around you. Just spending time with you is good enough for me. Hopefully, we will have many days like this."

Adrian was alluring. He knew how to bring out the butterflies in a woman. Jasmine may have thought of herself as one of a kind, but she was like most women when it came to being pursued by a handsome man. She was beginning to enjoy the chase. Although she was spiritually intrigued moments prior, she forfeited that spiritual encounter at the back wall to live in the moment. Adrian seemed to cloud her judgment enough to cause her to focus on her feelings for him, as opposed to the message God had for her in Jackson's artwork. It was a classic case of Satan's attempt to delete God's message before it could effectively impact her spirit.

As they continued to stroll through the exhibit, Adrian grabbed Jasmine's hand once again. He led her to one of his favorite pieces from Jabby's collection. This time when he touched Jasmine, she felt a chill shoot through her entire body. For a brief moment, her mind escaped to a place where Adrian was her man and she belonged to him. Likewise, Adrian noticed the pleasant look on her face when he touched her. As they stood in front of the piece, Adrian placed his right arm around Jasmine and pointed to the painting with his left hand in efforts to give his interpretation. Clearly, he was trying to test the waters and see if she would reject his advances. To his delight, Jasmine seemed to enjoy his touch. As the event came to a close, Jackson finally made his way back to his distinguished guests.

"Jasmine, I would like to thank you for coming out and supporting my event. Also, your dissertation on that one particular piece afforded me a very handsome offer. For that, I am eternally grateful!"

She smiled graciously and replied, "It was my pleasure, Jackson. I was captured by it and I couldn't help expressing how it made me feel. You are an amazing artist!"

Adrian smoothly shook his head in agreement as he added, "Jackson, I have a great idea. How about hiring Jasmine to attend your exhibits and create a buzz around your paintings like she did today. It'll be kind of like strategic advertising."

Jackson took a sip of wine and smiled as he placed his hand on Adrian's left shoulder. "That sounds great, my friend. However, what if some of the same collectors attend my exhibit in other cities and they feel they are being hustled by your uh, strategic advertising? No sir, I don't think so."

They all laughed in agreement as Adrian replied, "Yeah, I guess you have a point."

By the time Jasmine and Adrian exited the museum, it was hard to tell if they were friends or a couple. Adrian had his hand around her waist as they walked slowly toward the parking lot. Jasmine had fallen victim to the ambience. Once they found their vehicles, they stood silently gazing at each other. Adrian's lips slowly moved toward her lips. Initially, he thought she would stop him. However, the closer he got, the more confident he became. Jasmine peacefully closed her eyes right before she felt the texture of his lips. It started with a light peck and grew rapidly into a passionate French kiss. Adrian's heart fluttered with excitement as his mind scrambled in disbelief. As he held Jasmine tightly, her body began to feel like a jellyfish in his arms. The way he made her feel was incredible. The French kiss was followed by several wet kisses as they stared into each other's eyes. Adrian thought at any given moment, Jasmine would snap out of her trance and apologize for her actions and abruptly drive off in guilt and shame. However, it didn't happen that way. In fact, it was totally opposite. Jasmine whispered in his ear, "You are an incredible man. I am so glad I met you."

It was like music to his ears. He replied, "I feel the same way about you. I feel privileged to be in your presence. I can't help wanting more and more of you."

Jasmine's desires disregarded all the stop signs and red lights her spirit tried to place in her way as her flesh sat in Adrian's grip. The slow-pace friendship ended inside the museum. Outside the museum, things organically picked up pace to a speed Jasmine was foreign too, but obviously welcomed.

Before they began another round of intense canoodling, the sky began to rumble. In an instant, an untimely onslaught of rain ended their passionate embrace. As Jasmine opened her car door to escape being drenched, Adrian stood in the rain like a fictional character in a black-and-white movie. The rain seemed to provide a backdrop to intensify the moment. She smiled and said, "Go on and get out of this rain. We'll talk later. But I must say, you do look sexy standing there!"

Chapter 8

... Missing the Family

The west coast slowly became a familiar place for Michael. Everything was progressing smoothly. The execs were very pleased with the project being on time and on budget. Like every morning, he called his wife and had their usual conversation about the boys and what their workday would consist of, as well as their normal affectionate exchanges. Although Michael's professional career was on the upswing, he desperately missed Jasmine and the boys. After hanging up, he leaned back in his chair looking out of his window. He felt it was time to take Ms. Sprewell up on her offer to fly his family to the coast for a much-needed reunion. He yearned for Jasmine's touch. He also longed for the bond he shared with Brandon and Chris. The next morning, Michael sat in his office preparing to start another day of producing when Tracy stuck her head in the doorway and said, "Good morning, Mr. Man. How are you?"

Michael replied, "Oh, good morning, Tracy. I'm doing great. Just about to read my e-mails before I head to the studio and meet with the guys. Will you be coming through anytime today?"

Tracy answered, "I'm not sure if I will be able to drop in. I have a couple of meetings and a luncheon to attend."

"OK, that sounds like a full schedule! Look, when you get a minute, I wanted to call in on that offer you made to bring my family out to visit."

She replied, "Oh, that's not a problem. I was wondering when you would ask. Just let me know the dates and we will get on it. Hey, let me get up to the conference room before they start without me, but yeah, just get me the dates and we'll make that happen."

"Well, all right, sounds like a plan. Have a good one!"

Before breaking the exciting news to his family, he wanted to find out if Jasmine had any pressing issues at work that would spoil the surprise. He planned to set everything in motion once he figured out what days would be good for them to come. He couldn't wait to plan fun activities and make reservations to a couple of nice restaurants!

His morning began on a very high note. Later that evening, he called Jasmine and began to gather intel for their visit. When the phone rang, Jasmine was settling down for the night and anticipating Fletch's customary call. He began, "Hello, sweetheart, how are you?"

Jasmine sat comfortably on the bed with her legs snuggled under the covers as she answered. "Hey, Fletch, I'm good, sweetheart. Just got situated here at the house. Believe it or not, the boys are not bickering tonight, so it seems like it will be peaceful around here. How was your day?"

"Oh, just work, work, and more work. The project is moving along well, so I decided to head home earlier than usual."

The conversation continued pleasantly, as Michael found clever ways to get Jasmine to reveal her work schedule for the next few weeks. Voluntarily, she mentioned how she wouldn't mind a few days to get away from it all and just relax. The next morning, he began to put things in order. He didn't hesitate to consult the locals on where to go to impress his crew. Tracy and her secretary provided great suggestions. He wanted it to be a memorable time with his family. Michael even welcomed some tidbits from the elevator tech that serviced the elevators in the building. Michael greeted the tech as he worked. "Good morning. I guess I'll finally get my much-needed exercise using the stairs today."

The tech replied, "Good morning, sir. I should be done in a few minutes. Just running a couple of diagnostic checks. She'll be moving in just a moment."

"No, don't let me rush you. I'm pretty energized this morning. The stairs probably don't stand a chance. Um, if you don't mind me asking, are you originally from Los Angeles?"

The tech answered, "Born and raised!"

"Well, maybe you can help me. I'm Michael Fletcher and I actually live in Houston. My family is coming out to visit me and I wanted to take them to a very nice restaurant. I was wondering if you had any recommendations."

"Well, Mr. Fletcher, you've come to the guru of fine dining, considering I eat out a lot! If you really want to impress them, there are several upscale restaurants in Beverly Hills. The ambience and star power will be breathtaking for any out-of-town guest!"

Michael took mental notes and decided dining in Beverly Hills was the way he wanted to go.

As a couple of days went by, his plan began to take shape. All he needed was travel dates and it was time for liftoff. The kids had some time off from school coming up and he figured that probably was the best time to get them to come out west. Things seemed to be forming perfectly for Michael's family to finally be together again.

Meanwhile, Jasmine secretly continued to allow Adrian to become a part of her everyday routine. The more they talked, met for lunch, and took occasional walks in the park, the more she saw Adrian as a breath of fresh air. He slowly began to provide the fantasy experience.

As she was preparing to meet Adrian for a bite to eat, the music in her vehicle played the relaxing sounds of Luther Vandross. Jasmine loved the slow jams from all genres. Chris and Brandon always dreaded out of town trips. They knew their ears would curl up in displeasure as their mom sang background to every song. Her favorite crooner on the open road was the man himself, Mr. Frank Sinatra. While it was a far cry from the boys' hip-hop world, it was her escape to a world of romance, a time when men were gentlemen.

Unfortunately for Michael, Luther's sultry voice didn't tip the scale in his favor, as his wife's thoughts danced on visions of Adrian.

Shortly after she grabbed a table for two, Adrian arrived. He walked over with a huge smile on his face as if he had some good news. As he took his seat, Jasmine began to smile as well.

"Well, what's with the Kool-Aid smile, mister?"

Adrian responded, "Is it that obvious? So, I've been informed I have an offer on some commercial property I own in Florida. An investment group wants to lease the property. If everything goes as planned, I stand to make 400,000 dollars annually for the next ten years!"

"Whoa! Are you serious? When will the deal be finalized?"

Adrian continued, "We are set to close the deal in two weeks. Hopefully, everything will go as planned and all I will have to do is fly to Miami to meet the investors and ink the deal. Another reason for the smile is because I was thinking how wonderful it would be if I somehow convinced a certain someone to join me on a boring business trip to South Beach."

Jasmine blushed. Thoughts of a getaway instantly rushed through her mind. "Wow, I wonder who that certain someone could be. So how long would that certain person have to decide?" Adrian smiled once again and reached across the table. While gently wrapping his fingers around hers and slowly stroking the top of her hand with his thumb, he answered, "She has as long as she needs."

Once the lunch was over and they parted ways, the ride back to work was an interesting one to say the least. Jasmine considered all the questions that loomed in her head. "Of course, I can't go to Miami with him!"

"Wait, now, girl, are you actually considering passing up a getaway with a man like that?"

"How are you going to pull that off?"

"What if you are seen in Miami by someone who knows you and Michael?"

"How would you feel if Michael did this to you?"

"Well, how do you know he isn't doing it to you now?"

"How important is your marriage to you?"

"Maybe it will be OK, if you make it clear that you must have your own room."

"What's wrong with supporting a friend?"

The array of viewpoints occupied the entire drive. As Jasmine pulled into the parking garage, she assumed lead chair in her mental board meeting and decided to go with Adrian under certain conditions. With that in place, the meeting came to a close. Of course, she had no idea Michael was planning to bring the family out west.

A couple of days later, Adrian called Jasmine to get her decision. Oddly, her apprehensiveness from several days earlier was replaced with excitement.

"I hope you are ready to pack for South Beach. I will text you the dates a little later."

Jasmine responded, "Is that right? So I take it your certain someone has decided to join you."

"Well, I don't have a definite answer yet, but I'm confident she will join me. So what's it going to be?

She responded, "I think that certain someone is preparing as we speak to take some time off to support a lonely friend."

As Jasmine warmed to the idea of flying to South Beach with Adrian, Michael grew more and more excited about seeing his family! Undoubtedly, Mrs. Fletcher would soon have some decisions to make.

Jasmine knew she had to come up with a conceivable story to let Michael know she would be out of town. Her only viable option was to conjure up a phony business trip. She knew he would call while she was away, but that was something Adrian would have to understand when the time came to check in. She decided to give Michael a heads up on the so-called business trip once she had thought all the details through. Jasmine figured she had a couple of days to be deceitfully creative. While things were being arranged in her mind, Adrian sent the text message.

"Here are the dates for the trip. We will leave on the twenty-first and come back on the twenty-sixth.

I thought a couple of days to enjoy the city would be in order after conducting business. Pack light! That will leave room for all the things you'll bring home after we shop! LOL! Talk to you soon!"

In the meantime, Michael also had everything arranged and felt it was time to reveal the big surprise. As usual, the sun began to disappear and it was time for the distant lovers to hear the sounds of each other's voices as the evening came to a close. Jasmine and the boys were home for the night and the usual routine of eating, doing homework, and talking to the television during their favorite reality shows were in full swing. The phone rang and Brandon answered energetically. "Dad, what's up, big fella?"

Equally animated, Michael responded, "Hey, pal! It's so good to hear your voice. Yesterday, I called your cell phone and left a message asking you to call your old man."

Of course, Brandon came back with the typical teenager response, "I didn't have any missed calls from you and I rarely check my voice mail. My fault, Dad."

Michael just laughed because he understood teenagers. What Brandon actually meant was he was on the phone with a girl and things were going too good to interrupt, especially for a boring conversation with the old man. Brandon knew his dad was up on game, so he admitted, "All right, Dad, get off the gas. I'll answer next time. She was just too fine to leave sitting on the phone alone!" They both laughed as he handed the phone to Jasmine.

"Well, hello to you, my California love!"

Chris looked up from his leftover bowl of gumbo and commented, "B, did she just reference Tupac? She's lame!" The boys looked at their mom and shook their heads in disgust. Jasmine knew why they were shaking their heads and waved them off like flies as she continued with Fletch.

"Hey, baby! Look, I have a surprise for you guys. Put me on speaker." Jasmine's mind began to scramble in excitement as she told the boys to come near. Michael began to stutter as he rushed to reveal the big surprise. "Well, guys, it's been a while since we have actually been together. I'm very grateful to have such a supportive family. You all have been an inspiration to me. You've allowed me to pursue an opportunity I've always dreamt. I love each and every one of you for that. With that being said, I am at the liberty to fly you guys out west. And I'm talking first class. The label will pick up all expenses. So what do you guys say to that?"

Brandon and Chris were ecstatic! Jasmine seemed to be as equally excited. She instantly thought about strolling down Rodeo Drive with bags and bags of collectibles. It appeared she forgot all about her trip with Adrian. Well, at least until Michael began to run down the itinerary.

"Now, that's the response I was looking for! I was thinking you all would leave out on the twenty-first and return to H-Town on the twenty-ninth. That would give us an entire week to just run around the city and enjoy each other. Jasmine snapped back into consciousness when she heard the dates. Without verbally sharing her thoughts, she secretly pondered, "Did he just say the twenty-first? Oh my goodness!" She now had a real dilemma on her hands. Does she cancel with Adrian or should she try and ask her husband to change the dates? At that very moment, things became surreal. It was then she realized she was a married woman with feelings for another man. The fact that she was torn between pleasing Michael and keeping a promise with Adrian temporarily left her speechless. Without question, her excitement was violently replaced with an extreme case of anxiety.

It was time for an emergency conference. Jasmine needed input from qualified personnel and she needed it quickly. The only person she could call that would remotely understand her rapidly developing affair was her best friend, Paige.

Chapter 9

. . . The Choices We Make

———◆———

Time was ticking and Jasmine still didn't have a clue what to do. It seemed every hour on the hour either Michael or Adrian was calling with uncontrollable excitement. She repeatedly whispered, "What have I gotten myself into?" As she sat behind a wall of confusion, she wondered why Paige hadn't responded to her 911 calls for help. She needed her like yesterday. Feeling hopeless, Jasmine flopped back on the bed and stared at the ceiling fan with very little brain activity. The weight of the situation was just too much. As her eyes lowered for a stress nap, her cell phone began to ring. She jumped up and reached toward the nightstand, grabbed the phone, and anxiously examined the screen for the caller's name. To her relief, it was her mental paramedic, Paige! She answered frantically and began to rattle off the situation like a tattle-telling sibling.

"Girl, what took you so long to call me back? I'm in a big mess right now! I have no idea what I'm going to do. I know what's right, but I can't bring myself to disappointing him!" Jasmine provided no specific details to what she was talking about. It was a clear indication that she was mentally scrambled. Paige tried to listen and gather information, but Jasmine's words were vague at best.

Paige shouted, "Jasmine, Jasmine, calm down! Wait a minute! What are you talking about, girl?" Paige's call to attention seemed to work for the moment. "Now, I need for you to calm down and tell me what's going on. I won't understand anything if you're going to babble like you are losing your mind."

Jasmine's breathing slowed to a normal rate as Paige's composed disposition was that of a yoga instructor transferring her positive energy. "Whew, OK, girl, you're right. Let me calm down. Oh my goodness, I don't know where to begin. First of all, I haven't been completely forthcoming about my friendship with Adrian."

As Jasmine spoke, Paige's mouth began to slowly drop open and her eyes slightly squinted in a curious fashion.

Jasmine continued, "We've become kinda closer since the last time you and I spoke at the bistro."

"What do you mean when you say closer, Jas?"

"Well, we talk a lot and spend more time doing friend stuff. I mean close. Come on, do I need to spell everything out for you?"

Paige replied, "No you don't. But you do need to stop beating around the bush and tell me the truth. I mean the whole deep-rooted truth."

Jasmine didn't feel as comfortable as she thought she would be with telling Paige the truth about her feelings for Adrian. That was another sign that her flesh didn't want to be corrected. She really wanted Paige to offer solutions that would please both Michael and Adrian. She was losing precious time and she didn't want to hear any reproach.

"I understand, but it's hard to give the deep-rooted truth concerning Adrian because every day, my feelings reveal things to me. What I mean is, I didn't realize how I felt about him until the other day when he asked me to go to Miami with him to close a deal."

By the time Jasmine finished her sentence, Paige's mouth had reached full extension. Her eyes were no longer squinted. They appeared to be the size of full moons. She wanted to ask a slew of questions, but she figured it was best to let Jasmine get everything out before she chimed in.

"I'm going to be honest. I did accept the offer to go with him. At first, I convinced myself I was only going as a friend and nothing more. I see now that was a poor attempt to disguise my real feelings. I found myself looking forward to the trip. Then, out of nowhere, Michael called with his surprise. He wants us to fly out to Los Angeles and visit with him for a week. When he was explaining, I forgot about Adrian and was genuinely excited to take the boys out west. That's until he told me the dates. They coincide with the trip to Miami. Now, I'm faced with disappointing somebody. I know I should choose my husband, but I don't want to go back on my word with Adrian."

Paige wanted to choose her words carefully. Jasmine was her best friend and she cared for her like a sister. However, she knew her role was to say what was right and not what Jasmine wanted to hear. Honestly, she never feared Jasmine would fall victim to Adrian's lure the night they met. If any woman could turn away a man like that, it would be Jasmine. Her life is great. Her family is intact. She has a loving, hardworking husband, great kids, and successful career.

After processing her thoughts, Paige was ready to share. "Jas, first let me state the obvious. You are a married woman! This should not be an issue. You are not only a married woman, but you are a Christian woman. You and your family have been blessed in ways people dream of. I know you see how Satan is challenging your happiness. I know Adrian is an amazing piece of eye candy, but that's all he is in this situation. Now, tell me this. Is he worth your family?"

Jasmine sat in disgust. Her body was positioned like that of a chastised five-year-old. Instead of answering Paige's question, she sat in silence, which signaled for Paige to continue.

"I know when you are with Adrian, your flesh is on fire with excitement! Let's not ignore the fact that the man is a work of art. But I don't think he is worth hurting your family and restructuring your life for trips, dinner, shopping, and sex!"

Jasmine snapped out of her trance. "Whoa, wait a minute! I never said anything about sex. I have not had sex with that man! Don't assume stuff."

Paige answered, "Jasmine, listen. I didn't mean you've had sex already, but what do you think will happen if you go to Miami? Are you naive or are you in denial?"

Paige's response felt like a punch in the gut. She'd hit the nail on the head. Out of desperation, Jasmine blurted, "You just don't understand!"

Paige shouted, "Don't understand what? Oh, I don't understand your flesh is searching for a way to justify the lust you have for him? I don't understand your spirit has become weak? So weak, to where you aren't paying God any attention. I don't understand that in your mind, your way is better suited for you than His way? Let me ask you this. If Michael was home and you guys had that disagreement and you went out and met Adrian just like it happened, would you still be thinking about going to Miami?"

Jasmine responded, "Of course, not! Don't be silly."

"So basically, Adrian is replacing the companionship you lost when Michael left for California. Is that what you are saying?"

Jasmine replied, "I don't know, Paige. I don't know what is what right now. I just have to decide what to do about these trips."

Paige understood her assignment as a friend. Her job was to plant a seed in Jasmine's mind and not pound things into her. She felt Jas needed time to process. "Well, girl, I have some errands I have to run. I do pray you make the right decision. Personally, I think you should go and be with your family. They deserve that! Remember, either way, somebody will be disappointed. But you know who will hurt the most. Michael doesn't deserve your indecisiveness. You encouraged him to go, remember that."

Jasmine began to agree with what Paige had to say. The pep talk seemed to help her come to a decision. After Paige hung up, Jasmine prayed her feelings for Adrian would simply leave. However, she should have known Satan wasn't going to quit that easily. As she went to God, visions of his smile, his body, and the replay of the kiss in the rain competed with her utterance to heaven.

Shaking her head in disgust, she said solemnly, "It's so easy to hear God's word and vow to keep it until you are challenged to actually use it against what the flesh wants. What's wrong with me? I know better!"

She hopped from the couch and went to a shelf where she kept a notebook that contained notes from past sermons. She anxiously flipped the pages as she looked for a specific subject that addressed what she was going through. There was a sermon that talked about man being a tripart being. She needed to revisit the points that were made. She finally located the notes from Pastor Dixon's sermon and dove in like an Olympic diver. As she began reading the correlating scriptures, she remembered Michael always purchased a CD after every church service and placed them in a drawer. She rushed to the drawer and grabbed the CD and began to play it. Desperately seeking refuge, she began to listen.

We all have a body, soul, and spirit. Without question, your spirit is the top of the three. Our spirit connects us to God. I know some folks may disagree with me, but without that spiritual connection, you are not functioning as you were designed. Your flesh should be last in command and for good reason. I tend to believe the first to wither away should be the last to lead. Your spirit is designed to dwell with the Lord forever! Your body is just shaped dust that's destined to eventually return to its natural state. In my opinion, our selfish desires that cause problems in our lives can easily be traced back to the flesh being out of order. We tend to gravitate towards things that please our senses. Things that taste good, sound good, and definitely things that feel good. The soul is where your conscience, your will, and emotions are housed. Our passion, our drive, oozes from our soul! Whatever you do, be careful with your passions. It is a slippery slope. If your spirit is connected with the Father and pleasing him is priority, your passion will be in your Christian walk. In principle, if the flesh is running the show, passion will be used in all kinds of ways, depending on what you're into. And that's all I'm going to say about that. Basically, consider your soul as a free agent. It will follow whatever is in control of your being. With that in mind, I ask each and every one of you, "What's controlling you? What's in the driver seat? Are you headed to destiny or destruction?

Jasmine pushed the stop button and just sat in thought. She nodded her head in confidence as she stared blankly and whispered, "California, here I come." She felt a burden lifted. Listening to Paige and the CD brought her back to reality. She realized she tried to handle this with her head and not with the spirit. "Wow, what was I thinking? Adrian doesn't compare to my husband. That man has sacrificed in ways Adrian never could!" Jasmine seemed to have regained her consciousness. She didn't hesitate to break the news to Adrian. She felt it was only fair to let him know as soon as possible. Like a determined soldier, she walked to the bar to get her cell phone. As the phone rang, Satan worked at a feverish pitch to talk Jasmine out of her decision. However, she shot the devil down like a member of the Tuskegee Airmen. Absolutely nothing was going to stop her. After several rings, Adrian answered with a somewhat happy tone. The minute she heard his voice, her resolve seemed to take a hit and the determined pilot began to lose cabin pressure. Before she could get a word in, Adrian began to rattle off. "I was just about to call you. I just got off the phone with a close friend of mine in Miami, and she suggested I take you to the most amazing spa in the world. She said it is the place where the elite go to relax and be pampered. I want you to go to the Web site and take a look at it."

This definitely made matters worse for Jasmine. She closed her eyes, took a deep breath, and slowed her breathing. Thoughts of turning away from her resolve crossed her mind, yet she pushed forward.

"Adrian, I was calling you with a bit of bad news. I feel awful right now, but I'm afraid I will have to pull out from the trip. Some family issues have recently come up and I will be out of town during the dates we were to be in Miami." Although Jasmine made the right decision to be with her husband, she still pacified Adrian's feelings by not telling him exactly why she was cancelling. Maybe totally revealing her desire to be with her husband would cause him to seek friendship with another woman. She continued, "Adrian, I'm so sorry for causing you to lose money on airfare. I didn't see this coming and I apologize from the bottom of my heart. It's one of those things where you have no choice but to do what you have to do."

Surprisingly, Adrian's response wasn't what Jasmine anticipated. She expected for him to be upset and somewhat distant. However, his response was caring and understanding. "Oh no, I hope everything is all right! Don't worry about the trip. You go and do what you need to do for your family. The airfare is no big deal; I will call and get a voucher. I want you to go and take care of your business with a clear conscious."

Jasmine didn't realize at the moment, but neglecting to tell Adrian the truth actually opened the door for Satan to have an even stronger counter move to lure her flesh back into bondage. The two continued talking for another twenty minutes without Jasmine being pressured to reveal any pertinent information to her trip. Adrian didn't even ask where she had to go. The only thing he asked was when would she return home. Casually, Jasmine gave him her returning date and the chat gracefully continued until Adrian had to end the conversation due to an important incoming call. With that obstacle hurdled, Jasmine felt relieved and was able to concentrate on the family road trip to see Michael.

Chapter 10

. . . A Family Reunion

The big day had finally arrived. Jasmine and the boys were preparing to fly to Cali for the big reunion. The guys were very excited to see their dad and take part in the Los Angeles experience. They had already purposed in their hearts to pull no punches when they saw stars on the street. The goal was to approach the celebrities and take pictures with as many big shots as possible to boost their status with their circle of friends. Jasmine worked to put the finishing touches to her ensemble. When she stepped off the plane, she wanted to look like a movie star in her own right. Jasmine felt Michael deserved to have a gorgeous woman run into his arms after working so hard, all alone in Los Angeles.

"Guys, let's get out of here. Paige will be here in a minute. We're going to mess around and miss our flight!"

Brandon and Chris sat in the living room fully dressed, bags packed, and anxiously waiting for their mother to finally come down the hall. They both looked at each other and smirked when they heard Jasmine's all call. Brandon lowered his head and rubbed his face in irritation and sarcastically said, "Man, I hate when she does that! She says we are going to be late and she's the one messing around in the mirror. We all know that's her way of buying herself more time."

Chris laughed, "Yep, that's her."

Jasmine finally appeared as she walked quickly down the hall closing the clasp on her watch and putting on the tenth and final pair of earrings that won the right to be a part of the glamorous outfit.

Amazingly, they made it out of the house and Paige was able to get them to the airport in a decent amount of time. Once they reached their gate to depart, they had thirty-five minutes before boarding the aircraft. The boys began snapping pictures and making shout out videos to upload to their social media pages. Brandon began, "Yeah, it's your boy, B, about to head out west to see my dad. He is doing it big in LA right now producing a young hot artist! Stay tuned! I will post pictures and videos of my cohost and I as we add some H-Town flavor to the *City of Angels*."

Chris felt it was his time to introduce himself. "Hi, I'm your host C. Jizzle and let's talk to a few passengers as they wait to depart! Shall we?"

While clowning around with his brother, he noticed a very beautiful lady appearing to be in her midtwenties. She seemed to be entertained by their antics. Brandon gave his cohost the head nod to get her on camera. Chris didn't hesitate to follow his brother's advice.

"Hi, I'm Chris. My friends call me C. Jizzle and you are?"

She smiled and responded, "I'm Stacy."

As the camera continued to roll, she extended her hand and allowed Chris to politely grab it and respectfully place a gentle kiss like the perfect gentleman. It seemed to catch onlookers off guard. An elderly couple sat quietly as they observed the action and was reminded of a day when a young man knew how to properly greet a lady. The gracefully aged woman leaned toward her husband and whispered, "Now you don't see that anymore. I must admit it made me think of the day you kissed my hand for the first time." They both smiled and gave each other a quick peck.

Jasmine was ashamed by their TMZ impression and attempted to stop them, but they were in full swing.

"So, Stacy, will your stay in Los Angeles be business or pleasure?"

Once again, she smiled, positioned her hair, and played along. She looked into the camera and said, "Well, Mr. Jizzle, it's business and pleasure. I have a few early meetings, and then, it will be off to a meet and greet with my fans. Afterward, I plan to meet with my besties, for a girls' day at the spa."

By then, everyone were humored by the boys' ability to pass time with spontaneous entertainment. Jasmine helplessly shook her head. The lovestruck elderly lady complimented Jasmine on how delightful the boys were. Shortly thereafter, it was time to board the plane. The Fletchers took their seats and strapped in. The preflight filming seemed to tire out the guys. They slept most of the way, while Jasmine took several catnaps.

Once they touched down in LAX, Jasmine opened her eyes and saw the sun shine in a way she'd never noticed before. To everyone else, it was a normal sunny day. Perhaps, it was her emotions that heightened her attention to detail. Anticipating seeing her husband created a state of hysteria that caused her hormones to rush to her sexual gates. All she needed at that moment was Michael's hands around her. Thoughts of the intimate reunion caused her to squirm in her seat. Once the plane pulled into its assigned gate and the customary ding sounded to allow passengers to remove their seat belts and begin to disembark, she smiled and whispered, "This is going to be a great day!"

The trio meandered through the busy bodies that clogged the walking lanes in LAX and finally arrived at baggage claim. Brandon and Chris quickly spotted their luggage and it was time to start the festivities. They were expecting Michael to be standing there with a huge smile on his face to welcome them to California; however, he wasn't among the greeters. Jasmine felt a small amount of disappointment. She pictured her reunion with Michael would begin with a romantic airport hug and kiss. With him nowhere in sight, she feared it would not materialize. As they began to walk toward the exit doors, she noticed a limo chauffeur holding a piece of paper with the name Fletcher written on it. Her heart began to beat a little faster and her fantasy was alive once again. They approached the driver and introduced themselves.

"Hi, I'm Jasmine Fletcher. By any chance are you here for us?"

The gentleman smiled and politely responded, "I certainly am madam. This must be Mr. Brandon and Mr. Chris."

The boys were impressed. They felt they had status stepping off of the plane. He loaded their bags onto the cart and respectfully said, "Please follow me. Your chariot awaits."

Jasmine smiled. The two movie producers scrambled to find their cell phones to record another segment for their video. When the exit doors automatically opened, they instantly noticed the perfect horizon and beautiful palm trees that provided the cinematic backdrop for the occasion.

The chauffeur led them to a black Mercedes Benz limousine. From the appearance of the limo, nothing but the best is transported within its cabin. Before Jasmine could utter one word of admiration for their carriage, the rear door slowly opened and Michael exited the vehicle with a dozen of red long stem roses. When he stood upright, he appeared to be posing for a magazine. The boys began to run toward him with excitement. On the contrary, Jasmine slowed her pace to soak in the ambiance of it all. She wanted that moment to last as long as it possibly could. After exchanging hugs with his boys, Michael focused on Jasmine. He appeared frozen with watery eyes as he also enjoyed the slowed pace of Jasmine's steps. In a complete trance, he mumbled, "Excuse me for a moment fellas, I have a queen walking my way."

The long-distance lovers embraced with extreme passion. Jasmine buried her head into Michael's chest and found it very difficult to hold back the tears.

Once inside the limo everyone spoke at the same time, trying his or her best to take center stage. Michael leaned back and rested his head on Jasmine's shoulder with a huge smile on his face. It was obvious he was overjoyed with the family reunion.

"Babe to hear the sound of family is truly music to my ears. You never know what you miss until it's gone."

Brandon and Chris grabbed two glasses and gave their dad a head nod. Chris smoothly commented while reaching for the bottle of champagne, "I see you, Dad. Nothing but the best! Nice, my man!"

Michael played along with their antics and intercepted the bottle. "Well you know me. I had to do it big for my lady and my boys!" Michael handed Chris a fancy-looking container that resembled an expensive bottle of Petrus Pomerol 1998 while filled with some of Florida's finest. "For you two, I had to have the limo stocked with the good stuff. Knock yourself out with this freshly squeezed orange juice my brother. You're in Cali now! Handle your business and pour up!"

Not to be outdone by Michael's sarcastic attempt, the boys stayed in character. They opened the sunroof with their wine glasses and fancy orange juice bottle in hand yelling at cars in the other lanes. "Follow us! Pulp-free orange juice for everybody!"

Preoccupied drivers realized these two had to be from out of town. Jasmine covered her face as it filled with laughter. "Now, Fletch, you know it doesn't take much to get those two started!"

As they continued on the expressway, it was clear this family was special. Undoubtedly, they truly loved each other. It had appeared Jasmine had put Adrian completely out of her mind and consequently placed Satan underneath her feet. Michael got his family settled in and continued to play catch up. He didn't want to reveal everything he planned. He figured it would take away from the excitement each day would bring. After a long travel day, the quartet finished things off with a modest dinner at a local mom and pop diner Michael often patronized after late hours in the studio. The next morning, the sun shined brightly through the elongated windows. To Michael's surprise, the troops were awake and preparing to report for duty.

"Wow, I'm impressed! You guys never get up on your own. I thought I was going to walk in and see you two hibernating."

They were eager to see what their dad had in store for them. After breakfast, they all hopped into the car and began their first full day together. Fletch thought it would be fun to go to Venice Beach and rent some rollerblades. He felt the boys would get a kick out of the lively atmosphere while Jasmine would undoubtedly be intrigued by the shops that lined the beach. When he revealed his intentions, they all felt it was an excellent start to the day. Fully decked out with safety gear, Michael and Jasmine held hands while moving at a less than moderate rate of speed. They understood they weren't spring chickens and one fall could lead to surgery. On the contrary, Brandon and Chris refused to wear protective gear. They felt it would take away from their outfits. With the beach bunnies providing inspiration, they seemed to weave through traffic like Dale Earnhardt Jr. to get a better view of the beautiful cottontails. As predicted, Jasmine eventually, swapped the skates for shopping sandals and stopped at every other shop looking for that unique item she couldn't live without. Hours passed and they decided to get a bite to eat. The weather was ideal for lunch on the beach. Once consumption was complete, the breeze from the ocean accompanied by the sounds of the waves had Chris drifting off to la-la land. Brandon watched the surfers while music blared through his headphones. Michael leaned on his right side and stared at Jasmine. He enjoyed looking at her in all of her beauty, as the sun appeared to shine on her at the perfect angle. He couldn't help but utter sweet nothings to her.

"Hey, girl, I love you." Jasmine blushed as if they were on their first date. Michael always had a way of wooing her heart.

"Oh, sweetie, I wish we could stay with you until this project is over. I miss my husband, his touch, his eyes on me, and his way of making my body fill with tingles."

As Jasmine spoke, her eyes filled with tears. Michael loved his wife's response. He couldn't wait to surprise her with his plans for dinner. As the sun began its descent, they decided to head home to shower up and prepare to experience the west coast nightlife. Michael requested that everyone dressed very nicely. To their dismay, he wouldn't provide any information about the evening. Before long, they were riding on the expressway listening to Michael impersonate a tour guide as he pointed out places he saw celebrities. Thirty minutes later, Michael stopped the car in front of valet at one of the most prestigious restaurants in Beverly Hills. The ambience was nothing short of perfect. The boys appreciated the enormous black slate wall with alternating red, white, and green lights illuminating the calming water that overflowed into the retention pond. Jasmine knew her husband was putting his best foot forward. That's what always made Fletch a good catch. He had a way of showing how he valued relationships. He loved from the heart and thrived on making his family happy. The atmosphere of the dining area floored Jasmine. It was a very large area with each table displaying dressings fit for a presidential fund-raiser. Huge vases with red, yellow, and pink roses adorned the corners of the room. The domed ceiling displayed a Leonardo De Vinci–type painting that served as a great conversation piece. Beethoven's *Symphony 5* softly danced out of the speakers that were inconspicuously mounted in the walls to set the mood. The wait staff's tailor-made attire was impeccable. The patrons were treated more like distinguished guests. Jasmine commented on how it all felt more like a red carpet affair. Clearly, this was the best Beverly Hills had to offer. The maître d signaled for a waiter to lead the Fletchers to their table. Once they placed their orders, something amazing happened! Something you rarely see anymore. They actually had family time without being preoccupied with their cell phones. The night was reserved for actual conversation and laughter. Shockingly, Michael didn't have to insist. Without any extrinsic motivation, the boys felt social media was off limits. Michael made an excellent choice to impress his guests. For the Fletchers, their time together was priceless. Days later, the trip was narrowing down and the smiles of joy were giving way to looks of sadness. It was the last full day together. The boys knew it was almost time to leave their best friend. Michael tried to be encouraging, but it was obvious he was struggling himself.

"OK, guys, this is our last day. How about you two go and get ready for work."

Brandon and Chris looked at Michael with a confused look on their faces. Brandon asked, "Work? Dad what are you talking about?"

Michael snickered and responded, "Oh, I didn't tell you? Today, you two will be in the Busy Bee video shoot!"

The boys jumped up in excitement! Jasmine was caught off guard as well. She sat on the sofa with her feet tucked under the throw pillow, looked at Michael with a sexy smile, and shook her head as she thought to herself, "This man is full of surprises." The boys went to the room to change and Michael took a seat across from Jasmine.

"Now, what's that look for? You know I don't have time for that right now. I have to have the boys on location in a bit. Then again, if we hurry, we could probably…"

Before Fletch could finish, Jasmine cut him off. "Um, I don't want a quickie. Do you know who I am?" They both laughed as she continued. "No, I was just looking at you do your fatherly thing and it just made me think how I'm blessed to have you as their dad. And I admit, you kinda turn me on. I might have a little surprise for you later."

Michael stood up and walked toward her and leaned over to kiss her. "Well, in that case, I'll wait for my surprise. Now, will it be a little or enough to fill me up?"

Jasmine seductively answered, "Just make sure your hands are clean because you may fall asleep with your thumb in your mouth once I'm finished with you!"

Michael had a huge smile on his face. "So you plan on tucking me in with one of your adult bedtime stories?" He stood motionless looking at Jasmine in her volleyball shorts that exposed her sexy thighs. During that brief moment of silence, he allowed the heat in his body to build to a boiling point and playfully shouted, "Fellas, never mind! We just had a change of plans!"

Jasmine laughed and said, "Boy, stop, let me get dressed."

Once on location, the boys realized shooting a video wasn't a quick process. They were in several scenes and it required wardrobe and location changes that appeared to drain their energy. The director of the video noticed the boys' unenthusiastic demeanor and shot the scenes out of order to give them a break. He walked over to the depleted duo.

"Welcome to Hollywood, guys! This is the life everyone dream of and few are equipped to endure. I know that look. Seen it too many times before. Let me guess. When your dad told you about the video, your heart raced with excitement. Right? You thought this was going to be exciting all the way through. Unfortunately, the real excitement won't happen until the final edited version is plastered on screens across the world. Until then, guys, it's more like work. Grab something to eat and reboot. Four more scenes and you are done."

Brandon and Chris both nodded their heads signifying they understood. As the director turned to walk to his trailer, Chris being Chris said, "So was that his version of a pep talk? That didn't energize me. It made me sleepy."

They both laughed and continued clowning around while searching for food. Before long, the workday was over. Instead of going out for dinner their last night together, Michael and Jasmine thought it would be nice to stay in and have a home away from home kind of evening. An intimate night of movies and a home-cooked meal was on the agenda. Michael stood in the kitchen cutting onions and tomatoes for the masterpiece he was whipping up. The boys were doing what they do best as they both reached out to the masses of people on social media. Jasmine took advantage of her time and prepared a steamy hot bubble bath to sink into. While the setting seemed average, it was special for the Fletchers. Once her scene was set with candles and soft music playing on her cell phone, she stepped into tranquility. Jasmine's body was motionless beneath the bubbles, as she peacefully rested her mind. About an hour later, Michael lightly tapped on the door of the bathroom.

"Babe, the food is ready."

Jasmine remained still with her eyes closed and responded, "OK, I'll be out in a minute."

Before she began her exit from her pond of peace and relaxation, her phone began to vibrate on the vanity. Thinking nothing of it, she ignored the sound. She figured it was Paige texting to reconfirm the time she needed to be at the airport to pick them up. She began to dry off and noticed the message on the screen of her phone.

"Hope all is well. I haven't heard from you. Just wanted you to know the deal is complete!"

Clearly, Paige didn't send the text. Although the message was generic in content, it was enough to cause an unsettling feeling inside of her. Being with her family was her focus and Adrian's untimely text message presented a problem. Jasmine was irritated with the realization that the Pandora's box she allowed to open didn't magically close on its own while she was away on vacation. The Adrian situation, like all problems in life, seemed to have a supernatural ability to resurface immediately after coming down from a high of some sort. Jasmine quickly deleted the message without responding and continued to get dressed. She instantly snapped back into her previous mode and family night began.

Chapter 11

. . . Open Doors Cause Problems

A s they squinted their eyes to find Paige, she spotted them first and waved her hands to gain the trio's attention.

"Welcome home runaways!"

Jasmine responded, "Hey, girl, back to reality! No sooner than I got on the plane, I started thinking about washing clothes and going through a zillion e-mails from work. It was enough to make me stay with my husband in California."

Paige laughed, "Now, you knew it would be hard to leave that man. I know he pampered you like a newborn baby. I'm going to let you get home and settled. But tonight, I will come over so you can tell me all about it over a bottle or two of wine. Deal?"

Jasmine agreed, "Deal."

Once they got home, the boys were not thrilled that Jasmine had an incredible urge to clean the entire house. By their definition, the house was clean.

However, Jasmine was in the closet cleaning, baseboard wiping, garage-organizing mode. She began to reel off assigned duties like a drill sergeant. It frustrated the lazy teenagers. Just hearing the list of chores was enough to make them slump over in disgust. By the time the janitorial crew finished, it was almost dinnertime. Jasmine was too tired to cook, so when the boys suggested ordering pizza, she agreed.

"You, guys, order the pizza. I'm going to take a shower. Paige should be here in a bit."

Later, there was a ring at the door. Paige and the delivery guy arrived at the same time. She went ahead and paid the driver and stood with the box of pizza and a couple of bottles of adult beverages.

Chris opened the door with money in his hand, "What's up Aunt Paige? Oh, you brought pizza? We already ordered one."

"No, baby, I saw the delivery guy and paid him. Who was paying for this, you or your momma?"

Chris replied, "Oh we were paying for it."

Like all good aunties, Paige picked up the tab. "Well in that case, I got it. Keep your money, sweetheart. Now, if your momma was paying, that cow would have to reimburse me."

Jasmine was walking down the hall.

"I heard what you said, heifer."

Paige laughed as she looked for the corkscrew. Jasmine sat in her favorite corner of the couch and began her customary tuck of the feet under the pillows. That was her signal that she was totally comfortable and ready for gossip time. She told the boys to take the box of pizza to their room. Brandon looked at Chris and murmured, "You know they are about to talk about some stuff we are not supposed to hear, because she's letting us eat in the room."

Chris made eye contact with his mom and nodded, "Um-hum, she think she's slick. Just know we will be listening for the juicy parts."

Jasmine playfully threw one of the pillows at him. "Don't play with me, boy. You better get out of here before I get a hold of your juicy part and whip your butt!"

Paige also knew if Jasmine cleared the room, it was going to be more than a recap of her trip. "Tell me now. Will we need both bottles tonight?"

Jasmine took a deep breath, raised her eyebrows, and had the look on her face that nonverbally conveyed, "Oh, yes, ma'am!" While taking a slow sip of nectar and simultaneously shaking her head, she verbalized, "I think we will Love. I think we will."

Paige began to get up from her spot on the floor that most women find suitable for top-notch gossiping and headed for the second bottle. "Lord, now if you want me to counsel tonight, turn my wine to water, so I can help this child. I knew I had a purpose this evening. I just felt it."

Jasmine began to tell Paige about the trip and how Michael made them feel like royalty. She went on and on about the emotional high she experienced with him. Paige listened with a smile on her face asking detailed questions to probe deeper into her experience. All the while knowing her friend had a curve ball coming, she prepared herself for the counseling session.

"Paige everything was so perfect until last night. A text came through and it was you know whom. I can honestly say I never gave Adrian a thought the entire time. Even when the text came through, I wasn't moved in any kind of way."

Paige quickly interjected, "What did it say?"

"Oh, it wasn't much. He was just saying his deal was complete. Nothing big. I read it and deleted it and kept moving. I never responded. But on the flight home, I started feeling a little guilty about it. I could at least have said something to congratulate him. I noticed the closer I got to Houston, the jitters of Adrian began to build and that made me wonder what in the hell is going on with me?" Jasmine shook her head in confusion and took another sip.

Paige listened and processed before saying anything. Just before she could utter a word, Jasmine started up again. "I know what you are going to say. I'm suffering from the typical out of sight, out of mind thing. But I'm thinking it's something else. Oh, I forgot to add this. I turned my phone back on when we landed and I had a voice mail from Michael and a long text from Adrian. He was saying how he felt I was trying to send him a message by not contacting him. How he probably need to step back from the friendship because I didn't respond to his good news and things like that." Paige continued to listen and returned her thoughts.

"Tell me this was refusing to text him back because you are really trying to move away from that situation or because you felt Michael deserved your undivided attention at the time? 'Cause I have to be honest. Sounds like you didn't tell him the real reason why you couldn't go to Miami. If you truly wanted to stay away from him, you would have told him the real reason you couldn't go. I'm not trying to hammer you, but you know how I am when it comes to this kind of stuff. You are trying to put a Band-Aid on a wound that will continue to bleed until you sew it up. Do you really think this is just going to go away by ignoring him? Let's be honest, Jas, Adrian isn't just going to disappear. The longer you leave the door open, the harder it will be to close. Don't get upset with me, but you let that man get too close."

Jasmine sat speechless. She didn't mean for it to happen that way. After having such a great time with her husband, she couldn't believe how quickly Adrian resurfaced in her mind.

"OK, I admit I enjoy the attention. I'm really trying to stay away, but I don't want to be mean to him either."

Paige nodded, "I hear you, but you sound more like you are dieting and trying to stay away from sweets. At the end of the day, you don't owe him anything. If you just tell him and take away his options, you will control the situation and he will probably try to stay away from you as well. That's not being mean. That's being a faithful wife. The reason you are straddling the fence is because you are trying to make a decision with your emotions. In other words, you are juggling feelings for two men and not focusing on your love for God. Until you do that, you will fall deeper into your web of despair."

As usual, Jasmine internalized what Paige had to say. Her friend's words normally aided in resetting her course of action, but this time was different. She heard and agreed, but it didn't stick. Perhaps, the warning signs didn't stop her because Adrian indirectly resurrected a character flaw that had been operating incognito for a very long time.

The chatting continued until the bottles of wine were completely empty. Their eyes closed and the only sound that came from the family room was the ceiling fan. Jasmine's rest period was short-lived as her phone awakened her. When she was able to focus, she realized Adrian had sent another text. Before reading it, she placed a blanket over Paige and went to her bedroom. She sat on the edge of the bed and began to whisper the message out loud.

"Jasmine, I apologize for texting you this late, but I had to get this off my chest. I feel you are avoiding me. I really don't know why, but I have my suspicions. I'm only a friend and by no means do I feel you owe me anything. However, I do feel if you have a change of heart toward this friendship, I at least deserve to be told. If you don't respond this time, I will let your silence serve as your answer to cut any and all ties. With that being said, I hope to hear from you."

Jasmine sat and realized she was right back where she was before deciding to go to California. The only difference is now she had to make a decision to leave Adrian alone completely or continue the friendship. Here was her way of escape. This was her chance to end this without uttering one word to him. However, the more that thought loomed, the more she became helpless to her flesh. "Adrian is a good guy. What's wrong with having a friend to talk too?" She climbed under the covers, laid in a fetal position, and responded to his text. "Hi, Adrian. I apologize for not responding. I need to be honest with you. I didn't exactly tell you the complete truth about why I couldn't go to Miami. My husband planned to fly us out to Los Angeles for a vacation and it just so happened the dates clashed with your Miami trip. He told us after I had already agreed to go with you. I should have been upfront, but I didn't know how to tell you." After pressing send, she waited for his response. Several minutes later he replied, "Jasmine, I understand and had I known, I would have felt better about not hearing from you. I understand you are married with obligations. I'm not the guy that will get in the way of that. I guess at this point, I need to know where this friendship is going."

Jasmine sat without a response. She didn't know how to answer this man. He basically said he would be there if she wanted him there. It was evident Adrian wasn't going to magically disappear like Paige said. The ball was in her court. She needed more time to think. Using the late hour as an excuse, Jasmine evaded the question and asked if they could discuss it some other time.

The next morning while sitting in traffic, she decided to call Adrian and answer his question. Adrian energetically answered on the first ring. "Well, hello!"

Jasmine replied, "Well, good morning. I didn't expect you to answer. I was actually preparing to leave a voice mail."

Adrian answered, "No need for that now. You have my attention, ma'am. What's on your mind?"

Jasmine was about to make a huge mistake. She should have checked her manual, where *Christian Living 101* suggests "Never allow Satan to set the parameters in your life." Without regard, she chose to give Adrian an opportunity to come up with a game plan to stay in her world.

"I was thinking about our conversation last night and I have a question for you. How exactly do you think we can be friends and not cross the line? I mean, although we technically crossed the line the day we left the art museum." Jasmine wanted to hear something that remotely sounded like a solution. More specifically, Jasmine wanted Adrian to convince her that keeping him around would not be a threat to her marriage. Adrian was thrown off guard. He didn't expect to answer a question like that first thing in the morning. He paused, knowing he had to be very careful with his response.

"Well, first, let me address the day we stood in the rain. Emotions were racing and I felt so close to you. Admittedly, I allowed myself to see you more than a friend. I fantasized you being much more. I have to keep it real. Kissing you ignited a fire inside of me. But I realize that can't happen if we intend to remain friends. I value you as a person and your presence means a lot. I at least want to keep that. If not going there will afford me a friendship with you, I'd rather not go there and have you in some capacity. I think we'll be able to continue our friendship as long as we police our feelings. You know, I guess life has a way of working out."

Before Jasmine could respond, Adrian continued. "Could you imagine the pressure we would have put ourselves under, had you gone to Miami with me?"

While sitting in traffic, she felt his skeleton plan was enough to continue their friendship. Truth to the matter, Adrian didn't provide much of a plan at all. It was obvious, Jasmine's flesh was weakening and it caused her to settle for the same type of words he gave before their first kiss at the museum. For the next several weeks, they met for lunch and talked on the phone. Slowly, the relationship became stronger than before. As a result, Jasmine only told Paige the things she knew wouldn't set off a lecture on doing the right thing. Paige noticed Jasmine hadn't mentioned Adrian. She felt her friend either resumed a life of wholesome living or she was intentionally keeping her out of the Adrian saga. She became saddened with the thought of her best friend excluding her from her life in fear of any judgmental opinions. Paige wondered how to address what she was feeling. Like any typical day, she called Jasmine to gossip, only this time she planned to slip in a conversation about Adrian. Paige knew timing was everything. Her transition to Adrian had to be within the flow of the conversation.

"What's going on, chick? I called you yesterday and sent two text messages and you didn't respond. Are you acting funny?"

Jasmine responded, "Now you know better than that. I meant to call you back when I got settled and lost track of time. These kids were getting on my nerves, and by the time I took a shower and talked to Michael, I fell asleep. What's going with you? What did you need?"

Paige answered, "Oh, I just wanted to see if you wanted to attend an expo that's being held at the convention center next week. I had an extra ticket and it would be a good day date, especially since you have been avoiding your sister."

Jasmine knew she was avoiding her best friend and desperately wanted to talk to her without judgment. "OK, I am going to tell you something, but you have to promise you aren't going to start preaching and opening the doors of the church on me. I just need you to try and put yourself in my shoes."

Paige replied, "So basically you are saying for sake of conversation, watch my Jesus talk?"

Jasmine began laughing, "Um, yeah that's what I'm saying. I just want you to hear me as a woman with emotions, not as a married mother of two. Can you do that?"

Paige paused and humorously answered, "I'll try, but I can't promise you nothing."

Jasmine continued laughing, "Well, try real hard this time."

Paige was relieved she didn't have to find a way to bring Adrian up in conversation. Her challenge was to listen to Jasmine while struggling with the compulsive urge to take over the conversation and offer advice. She began to explain her continued struggle with Adrian and surprisingly, Paige listened without interruption. Playing the role of a therapist, she easily diagnosed her patient. As she made mental notes, Paige feared this would eventually end with someone getting hurt. She decided the best thing to do was to be there for her, but pray God open her eyes before things spiraled out of control.

Chapter 12

...In Too Deep

———— ◆ ————

Michael's stint in Los Angeles had reached its midpoint. Things were going better than expected and there were talks of extending an offer to him to be a part of the label's in-house production team. His career was heading to heights he'd never imagined. Although he was thankful for the opportunities to advance his career, he missed his family greatly! He had mentioned to Busy Bee's manager that he felt a void in his life without his family and there had been times he just wanted to pack up and go home. Michael's connection with Jasmine ran deeper than cliché love a husband usually has for his wife. He often told people he married his best friend. While Jasmine shared the same sentiments of sorts, her faithfulness to Michael was being compromised.

Jasmine's workload was becoming overwhelming. It seemed to be project on top of project and meeting after meeting. Deadlines caused her anxiety levels to shoot through the roof. It got to a point where all she wanted was an entertaining happy hour to take the edge off! A colleague recommended an upscale happy hour spot where many professionals gathered to drink their deadlines and mergers into oblivion. Midtown had quickly become executive row. It was a place where an intellectual could hang loose like a college kid at a frat party. It wasn't long before Jasmine had become a sorority sister of this establishment. Paige joined her from time to time when her schedule allowed. Usually, Jasmine wouldn't think of venturing out alone, but things were changing. An after-five therapy session quickly became her norm. On some occasions when Paige couldn't join her, Adrian dropped in for a session of drinks and conversation. One particular Friday, Jasmine walked in heading to her favorite section at the bar and noticed a man from a distance that resembled Adrian. She thought it was odd. Adrian usually waited for Jasmine to give him the *all clear* to join her. She was very careful not to have him cross paths with Paige. However, this day was different. It was indeed Adrian sitting in a defeated position with his head hanging in despair. Jasmine wondered if he had too much to drink already. When he lifted his head, she quickly realized he wasn't intoxicated at all. His eyes were blood shot red and he had a very helpless boyish look on his face. Jasmine quickly placed her hands on each of his shoulders, leaned over to a face-to-face position, and looked with a sincere concern.

"Adrian, what's wrong?"

He heard her, but he couldn't manage to say a word. He sat there with a blank look on his face. She shook him and tried again, "Adrian, what's wrong?"

This time, he responded with a faint voice, "She's gone. My mother passed away."

Jasmine sat in the bar stool next to him without anything to say. She didn't expect to hear that. For a few moments, there was nothing but silence. She didn't know enough about Adrian and his family to feel comfortable with probing deeper. Equally, Adrian didn't feel close enough to Jasmine to open up the full array of emotions that wrecked his heart and mind. Therefore, they both sat staring in opposite directions. Adrian was filled with heartache, while Jasmine searched for something to say. She felt out of place sitting next to a man she has developed feelings for, yet realizing she really didn't know enough about him to effectively console him. While sitting there, she quickly had a vision of Paige speaking to her. "Jasmine, how do you feel now? We both know you shouldn't be here."

Suddenly, Adrian broke his trance, placed his hand on hers and said, "I just don't know where to start. I have so much to do in order to give her a proper burial. I feel so weak. I don't have anyone to help me get through this. Just the thought of going home alone hurts."

Jasmine didn't understand what he meant by that statement. Adrian continued, "I don't think I told you, but my mom was living with me the last four years because of her health. To go back home, knowing she's no longer here seems unbearable. I feel I'm in a bad dream and I can't wake up. This can't be really happening!"

Jasmine began to think about how she felt when she lost her grandmother. Her emotions overwhelmed her when she received the news while away at college. She also remembered how every girl in her dormitory stood in solidarity on her behalf. Their resolve to get her through a tough time played a huge part during her grieving process. Needless to say, Jasmine and Adrian's experiences were polar opposite. Adrian felt like an abandoned kid in need of a consoling hug, the type of hug that said, "I'm with you until your pain is completely gone." At that moment, he felt Jasmine was the only woman with that ability. He just wanted to fall into her arms and allow her touch to calm the frenzy in his head. The longer they sat glued in place, the more Jasmine felt an obligation to comfort him. The longer she looked at the pain that blanketed his face, the stronger the urge got to hold him. He wanted what she pondered on giving, and finally, Jasmine stood up and gently turned his swivel barstool to center his body with hers. She then gave him the hug he secretly desired. On cue, Adrian's eyes slowly closed as he rested his head on her chest for a brief moment of serenity. As she held him, she wondered if she could actually help him get through this ordeal. By the way he held on, it was clear she was someone he wanted to lean on. After embracing, the bartender came over and placed two of their favorite concoctions in front of them. He gently touched both of their hands simultaneously and said, "The first of three rounds on the house!" Joe was the preferred bartender on Friday nights because he had a knack for connecting with the regulars like family. Adrian and Jasmine both thanked him for his contribution in efforts to connect with Adrian's pain.

As the evening went on, Jasmine settled into her role and Adrian began to laugh more as he told stories of his mother. Before long, they both were beyond their usual limit of beverages; and once again, Adrian's mind slipped back into a somber state. The thought of going home was terrifying. Jasmine was caught off guard with Adrian's next question. His words were slightly slurred as he made an appeal.

"I hope I'm not out of line asking you this, but is there any chance that you could stay with me tonight? I mean, just to keep me company."

Although Jasmine was shocked with his request, she didn't show it. Before speaking, she subconsciously prepared an answer. "Adrian as much as I would love to be there for you, I don't think that's a good idea for obvious reasons." That seemed like the perfect response. However, Jasmine quickly considered a second draft before officially answering. "Honestly, Adrian, I don't see how one night would help you. It will only give you a false sense of security. We both know I can't be there every night to help you through this." She decided on the second response because she felt it wasn't as abrasive. She should have actually gone with option one to have Adrian focused on the fact that she was a married woman. By choosing option two, she allowed Adrian an opportunity to be persuasive and once again talk her into it.

"No, I think you are misunderstanding. I know you can't be there for me every step of the way. It's just, the first night probably will be the toughest, and I feel you being there would help me get through it."

Not only did the alcohol affect her inhibition, it ignited the curiosity of probing a little deeper into the world of this gorgeous man. Ironically, while she deliberated, the boys called to ask if they could spend the weekend with Jason. After giving them instructions to lock up, she gave the OK. Adrian paid the tab and grabbed Jasmine's purse as she ended her call.

"So are we all set?"

She gave him a slight smile and nodded yes. After a thirty-minute drive, they finally turned into Adrian's neighborhood. She was welcomed with an elaborate fire and water show that entertained motorists as they entered the subdivision. It was a smaller version of what she had seen in front of the Mirage Casino in Las Vegas. The palm trees that lined the median gave the neighborhood a vacation feel. Every home seemed to be custom designed to the owner's expensive taste. Ironically, the elaborate setup didn't help Jasmine's condition. She felt butterflies dance around her stomach when she pulled into Adrian's driveway. She thought, "Lord, what am I doing? This is not where I'm supposed to be." Satan had an agenda and he could not allow her to have a conversation with God. Before she could hear His voice, Adrian got out of his car and shouted, "No, sweetheart, park in the garage!"

A subtle distraction caused Jasmine's intended dialogue with God to be reduced to a brief anticlimactic monologue. It was a clear example of a person diagnosing a problem within and not staying dialed in long enough to receive instructions to solve it. He waited by the garage door.

"Come on, let me give you a tour of my humble abode."

On the contrary, Adrian's home was not a typical house. Upon entry, Jasmine struggled to keep her jaw from dropping. She knew he was well off, but this house boasted a larger portfolio than she imagined. Every piece of art seemed to have once decorated the walls of museums and galleries. Adrian grabbed her hand and led her to his favorite room in the house. Jasmine wondered if this was his power move to get her into his bedroom. However, he took her to a room she never imagined he would find solace. Before entering, he turned to her and said, "I want you to know once we get inside, I intend to get you out of your clothes."

Jasmine's eyebrows rose as she replied, "Whoa, so just like that? You think your low voice and…"

Before she could finish, he laughed and opened the door. When she looked inside, her confusion quickly turned into concern. The room resembled the workshop of a dedicated seamstress. Female mannequins lined the perimeter of the oversized room. All were adorned with outfits that caught her eye. She didn't know whether to question Adrian about what seemed to be a weird fetish or begin shopping.

By the expression on her face, he could tell Jasmine was puzzled.

"I guess you are wondering what in the world is all of this? Let me explain. My mom made her own clothes for years. Some of the artwork you saw coming in were some of my pieces. As a kid, I would draw basic sketches of clothes and Mom would take it and bring it to life. She loved sewing and I loved providing the ideas. Before long, she was teaching me how to make dresses, suits, and the whole nine. It became a serious hobby when I actually sold a dress to a lady that was bombarded with compliments. Since then, I've designed and sold hundreds of pieces. I've found women will spend a pretty penny for unique designs."

Jasmine responded, "You don't have to tell me!"

Adrian began to slip back into depression as he spoke of his mother. His eyes began to water, "Jasmine, my mom and I were very close. That woman thought me a lot about what a lady likes. So that brings me to asking you to remove your clothes and do me the honors of trying on this dress I made especially for you. If you like it, it's yours! So please, enjoy. I'll be back."

Jasmine put the dress against her body while looking in the mirror and turned in a circle like Cinderella. Once she put it on, she was floored by the precision in which Adrian cut the dress. It hugged her curvaceous body as if he measured her beforehand. She was flattered that he memorized every inch of her body to create such a fashionable masterpiece. From the other side of the door, Adrian asked for permission to enter. When he saw her in the dress, he stopped in his tracks and uttered, "Damn!"

Feeling sexy as hell, Jasmine replied, "You and this dress make me feel amazing!"

The heat in the room instantly began to rise as they walked toward each other with seducing eyes. Jasmine grabbed Adrian and pulled him into her and began kissing him passionately! Their tongues were intertwined for what seemed to be an eternity. Their hands were being entertained by the contour of each other's body. Jasmine rubbed up and down Adrian's muscular shoulders and back as if she was reading braille. Likewise, Adrian caressed her back up and down until he reached her voluptuous backside. He couldn't believe how perfectly the combination of muscle and well-placed fat cells formed curves that filled every centimeter of his masculine hands. He couldn't help but take a break from kissing and help-lessly whisper, "Your ass feels so good in my hands! I want you now!"

Needless to say, Jasmine wanted Adrian as well. While unbuttoning his shirt, she whispered in his ear, "Take me."

The goal was to make it to the bedroom. While softly kissing on her neck, Adrian stood behind Jasmine and slowly ushered her down the half-lit hallway. In order to get to the master bedroom, they had to walk through the great room. Adrian's sec-ond favorite room featured ocean view windows that opened to the backdrop of an infinity pool and land-scaping that would make a Hawaiian island envious. Perfectly placed speakers embedded in the walls cooed the smooth jazz sounds that made it impossible to escape. The pool lights indirectly created the perfect lighting for the great room. The ambience of the room caused her body to be invaded with chill bumps. She quickly turned around to find Adrian's button-down shirt was hanging off his shoulders exposing his chiseled pecks and abs. Jasmine bit her lip and gripped his head and began round two of kissing. It was obvious the comforter and pillows in the bedroom would remain intact. That night, the great room became a great room for long awaited, passionate sex. In seconds, they both stood completely nude. He laid her on the custom-made chaise and slowly entered her body. At the very moment he entered her, she officially entered the forbidden land of adultery. It was clear Jasmine Fletcher was in too deep.

Chapter 13

. . . Safety in Numbers

A couple of weeks passed after Jasmine's escapade with Adrian. The first four days were filled with guilt. She couldn't believe she actually committed adultery. Thinking of all the warning signs she ignored caused her to sink to an all-time low. By week two, she convinced herself it was a terrible mistake and it would never happen again. Deep down, she felt Michael's homecoming would calm the turbulence in her life just like his presence did the trick in Los Angeles. She was certain when that time came, Adrian would understand and bow out like a gentlemen. Although it was a struggle, she found a way to file her transgression away into the **Never Again** folder.

It was a typical Saturday morning for the Fletcher trio. A day of cleaning, washing clothes, and running errands was on slate. Ironically, Michael called to tell Jasmine the project was wrapping up and he would be home for good soon. She became excited to finally have her husband back. However, Jasmine's excitement was short-lived. Satan wasn't done with her. Her mind began to seesaw like a child on the playground. The thoughts of her adulterous evening proved to be more resistant than she fathomed. While folding clothes and watching television, her mind began to drift back and forth from Adrian's touch to Michael's return. She found herself in a mental wrestling match. Eventually, her thoughts of Adrian gave way as she gravitated back to the great room. She sat dazed as she envisioned how Adrian kissed and nibbled all over her neck and how he skillfully utilized slow long strokes while staring into her eyes to hypnotize her body to move her hips in unison. It wasn't sex. It was more like a connection. Her flesh began to heat up just thinking about it. Then, the notion hit her. "Damn, how am I going to walk away from him?" She grinned when she thought of what Adrian said about his mom teaching him what a lady likes. Jasmine whispered out loud, "Great job, Momma! Your son got skills!" Before she drifted deeper into the highlights of that night, the doorbell interrupted her thoughts.

"Chris, get the door!"

When he opened it, Paige greeted him and walked in dressed for shopping.

"Hey, girl! Get dressed, let's move around today."

"Well, hello, Ms. Paige! Why didn't you call me and give me a heads up?"

Paige replied, "I did, heifer. You didn't answer your phone."

Jasmine picked up her phone and saw three missed calls from Paige and one from Adrian.

"Oh no wonder, my ringer was off. I see you are all animated today. But before you start naming a thousand things you want to do, FYI, I'm not trying to go and spend a bunch of money. I know how you get when you are in the shopping mood."

Paige raised her designer shades high enough to expose her eyes. "Um, who said you were going to have to spend anything? Maybe I wanted to be a blessing today. See, you can't be nice to heathens!" They both laughed.

"Girl, whatever! You like to spend and you can do that with the money you make and no children."

Paige answered, "Jasmine hush! You make more money than me and your husband is this big music producer now. Don't start with me. Anyway, I was thinking we could stroll through the Galleria and get lunch at that new restaurant on Westheimer and gossip. I have some exciting news to share."

Jasmine energetically grabbed the folded clothes and headed to the room to get dressed as she humorously mumbled, "Stroll through, this girl know she doesn't stroll through malls. More like camp out."

Paige shouted, "I hear you. Just hurry up and get dressed!"

As Jasmine predicted, Paige didn't stroll through the mall. She wanted to stop in every single store. Jasmine wondered why she frantically looked for the perfect outfit and shoes. It seemed nothing was good enough. Jasmine finally asked, "What are you looking for exactly? You've tried on several outfits and shoes I think looked great on you. Something is up!"

Paige gave a devious smile as she walked into yet another store and replied, "Maybe."

Holding true to form as a best friend, Jasmine's fashion juices began to flow because she sensed Paige has finally met her a showstopper! Jasmine warned, "Ooh girl, you better tell me everything when we get out of here or I'm going to hurt you!"

The shopping continued, and finally, Paige found a dress that suited her taste in ways that made her smile from ear to ear. Walking out of the dressing room, she enthusiastically screamed for Jasmine to stop trying on shoes and come see her selection. Hearing Paige's stress call, Jasmine flagged a salesperson.

"Excuse me, sir, can you take this to the register and keep these Christian Loubies under lock and key. I will be purchasing this perfection of a shoe! I have to go and calm down a hysterical customer."

When Jasmine saw Paige, she stopped and smiled, "What in the hell? Girl, are you going on a date or getting married? You look like a movie star in that dress!"

"So just in the dress? I don't look like a star without it? So you saying it's a big drop off when I take it off? Don't say it like that 'cause I don't want it if I have to sleep in it to be stunning."

Jasmine laughed, "Paige shut up. You know what I meant. Finally, this girl has found the eye-popping dress for her mystery man!"

Paige couldn't stop blushing as she turned in a circle while looking in the mirror. Watching her spin quickly took Jasmine back to Adrian's sewing room and the emotions she had when she tried on the dress he made. She appreciated Adrian even more, considering Paige went on an all-out search to impress her new friend and Adrian actually created something for her with his magical hands.

It took everything Jasmine had to fight back the urge to tell her secret. After making their individual purchases, it was time to eat and share. With these two ladies, the keywords for professional caliber gossip were location, location, location! The new restaurant Paige wanted to try was the main feature of the new high-rise condominiums that upgraded Houston's Galleria area. It sat on the top floor of the twenty-five–story building as it overlook the city.

"All right, start from the beginning. Who is it and how did you meet?"

Paige enjoyed holding Jasmine in suspense. "Whoa, slow down. Can I order a drink and appetizer first? My goodness!"

"Paige stop playing and come on with it. You're making me mad now!"

Paige ignored Jasmine's last comment and finished ordering drinks and appetizers. "OK, I met him at church. He just moved here from Chicago and was visiting for the first time. I don't know if I told you, but I'm an usher now. When they asked for all the visitors to stand, he stood up. When I saw him, I almost got dizzy. Girl, God said, 'That's him!'"

With a playful smirk on her face, Jasmine asked, "So God told you he was the one while you're supposed to be focused on ushering? So basically both you and God were off task, playing love connection."

Paige popped her hand to stop the sarcasm and continued, "He was about 6'2" Hershey brown and sexy as heaven!"

Jasmine's eyebrows raised, "Sexy as heaven? That's a new one."

Paige gave her a look like, "Do you want to hear the story or what?" She moved forward, "Anyway, I was on the other side of the church and we had to pass out the guest packages. The only visitors in my section were this old couple and, Lord forgive me, a man with looks that wasn't anything to talk about. While nobody was looking, I slid the packages I had under the seat and pretended I was out and walked to the back row to get some more. The whole time, my intention was to come up the aisle where he stood. It had to be nothing but God, because the girl who was working that area really ran out and was rushing to get another one to give to him. I could tell she had the same intentions I did, but the devil is a lie. I swooped up another guest package like it was a ground ball and I was playing for the Astros. I walked up the aisle like a good Christian woman, but with a little *ooh wee* to my sway. You know what I mean?"

Jasmine was dying laughing. "So you're in church clowning like you are walking the runway?"

Paige confidently answered, "Um, yes, ma'am! I wasn't playing! I told you what God had said. So I acted as if he was just another visitor when I handed him the bag. I didn't mind looking like I wanted a drink of water, but I couldn't make him think I was completely thirsty like some of these women out here."

Jasmine nodded in agreement and added, "Thirsty? Nowadays, some women on social media are more like dehydrated! Grown women with kids, twerking in the kitchen trying to catch a man. That's ridiculous!"

"Jasmine! You're talking about me staying focused. Listen. When he took the bag, he made sure he touched my hand. Then, he slid his hand all the way down and slowly rubbed my fingertips. Now, where I'm from, that means something. It was very subtle, like he didn't want the whole church to notice, but it was enough to say, 'I see ya girl!'"

Jasmine listened energetically as Paige's eyes lit up while giving an account of that day. "So I assume y'all hooked up after church."

Paige continued, "Well, not exactly. After church, I thought he would make eye contact with me, so I made sure I was in his line of sight. However, he was preoccupied with a couple that started talking to him as they walked out of the sanctuary. I quickly gave up on that fantasy and started jaw jacking with Lisa and Sister Abernathy. Girl, let me tell you about this old lady. Sister Abernathy is an elder in the church and is the head of the greeters and ushers. I didn't know it, but she saw me hide the guest package under the seat. She said, 'Baby, can I talk to you?

Now, I didn't want to say this in front of Lisa, but I saw what you did and I saw why. I just wanted to pull your coattail and tell you to be mindful of your duties in the Lord's house. With that being said, I must say, I don't blame you. Child, that man was as fine as my Herbert was when I first saw him. God rest his soul. You have to teach me how to walk like that so I can strut in when I go play bingo!' Jas, she had me rolling. I couldn't believe that saved and sanctified old lady trying to catch at the bingo parlor."

They both laughed at old Sister Abernathy. The waiter politely interrupted the ladies and placed the appetizer on the table. Jasmine knew there was more to the story, because hours earlier, she was on an all-out search for a ballroom dress as if she was invited to dinner at the White House.

"Something is telling me you have more to tell me."

Paige blushed, "I'm getting to that. Well, after talking with the ladies, I headed to my car. I just knew he was already gone, but when I walked out of church, he was in the parking lot still talking to the same people. He was facing my vehicle and when I opened the car door, I gave him one more glance. Girl, that was the best move I could have made. When I looked up, he was looking at me while trying to appear interested in the conversation with the couple. He waved and asked me to hold on and said he needed to talk to me. I'm not going to lie. I got excited and nervous all at the same time. As he walked over, all I could focus on was how handsome this man was. He introduced himself and we instantly hit it off. His name is Robert and like I said before, he's from Chi-town. He's been divorced for seven years and has custody of his sixteen-year-old son. He's an electrician and lives near the medical center. Ever since, we've talked or seen each other just about every day."

Jasmine looked shocked when Paige said they have been seeing each other for a while. "So let me see if I follow. Cow, you've been dating and I'm just now finding out about it?" They both giggled. "Well, I have an exciting announcement. My hubby will be home soon!"

Paige screamed, "Finally! Hey, that is perfect timing. I can introduce Michael to Robert. Hopefully, they will hit it off. 'Cause the only thing I'm concerned about is Robert's conviction to God."

Jasmine asked, "What do you mean?"

"Well, it's just he sometimes sounds like a skeptic instead of a believer. Almost like he goes to church to gather research instead of gain knowledge. Just seems he's afraid to totally surrender. Maybe being around Michael will clarify some stuff for him, especially if it's coming from a man. We all know there are a million women begging their man to come to church and give God a try. It's early and I don't want to seem like I'm being domineering."

Jasmine laughed and sarcastically replied, "Yeah, give the man some time. Lord knows your overbearing ways will come!"

Later that evening, Jasmine thought about her husband. She missed him and couldn't wait to hear his voice around the house. She also thought how Paige finding a man could help her transition away from Adrian and into doing couple activities. With that as an option, she became confident that she would resume being the wife she was before Michael left.

Three weeks passed and Michael was due to land in a couple of hours. It was enough time for Jasmine to drop the boys off at the barbershop for haircuts and get a manicure before his arrival. Jasmine was dressed in a sexy outfit to welcome her hubby home. It was like Michael was returning from battle.

When they walked into the airport, the feeling she felt when she went to Los Angeles came back. She couldn't wait to hug and kiss him. The boys were as equally excited. Before long, Michael appeared with a smile that would light the sky. Brandon and Chris walked over for a hug and a manly fist bump. As they grabbed his bags, Jasmine glided into his arms as she excitedly whispered, "Oh my God, my husband is home!"

The romantic reunion was sealed with a sample kiss signaling to him much more was on the way later that night. Instead of going out and extending the homecoming, Michael opted to stay home and grill steaks on the patio. Jasmine felt it was a perfect opportunity for Paige to bring her new friend to the celebration. She talked it over with Michael and he agreed. On the way home from the airport, she gave Paige a call.

"Hey, girl! What you doing?"

"Oh, just a little of nothing. I just got off the phone with Robert. Oh Lord, I can hear it in your voice, what you got going?"

Jasmine excitedly responded, "Well, I called to inform you that my man is officially home and we are having an intimate celebration at the house tonight. We are grilling steaks, and Michael and I wanted to extend an invite to you and your new something, something."

Paige laughed, "You and Michael want me to bring my something, something? More like you want to get all in my business! Girl, bye!"

"Well that too!" Jasmine admitted. "Get him back on the phone and tell him you've made dinner plans and we'll see you guys later."

Paige answered, "I guess. Look, don't try and act like my momma tonight. You know how you get with all your questions. Tell my brother welcome home and I look forward to seeing him tonight."

"All right, girl. See y'all a little later!"

Jasmine was excited about the possibility of doing the couples' thing. She felt it would aid in putting a distance between the unhealthy practices she fell victim to with Adrian. Michael settled in and had the grill emitting the savory flavor of oak wood into the air. Jasmine checked her phone before turning it off. The last thing she wanted was to get a random call from Adrian. Paige and Robert arrived and the evening had officially began. The atmosphere was festive. Paige gave Michael an enormous hug to welcome him home, while Jasmine was introducing herself to the newest addition to the fold. They all headed outside where Jasmine had things set up like an outdoor lounge. It was perfect for intellectual conversation.

Michael gave a brief recap of his time in Los Angeles in efforts to give Robert the floor. It wasn't an opportunity Robert necessarily welcomed, considering he didn't have much time to prepare for the evening. He was a tad bit nervous and began speaking with a slow calculated approach.

"Well, as you know, I'm Robert and I'm from Chicago. I've recently moved to Houston and it has been a transition, especially with the weather being very different from what I'm used to."

As he continued, he grabbed Paige's hand. "It wasn't until I met this lovely lady that the move started to make sense." As he went into detail, it was apparent he was beginning to loosen up. "I'm a divorcee and a father of a teenager. Making the decision to leave our roots was a difficult choice because it involved my son. As you would expect, he didn't want to leave his mom and friends. So it was a challenge to say the least. Eventually, he embraced the change after I struck a deal that will cost me a car his senior year. Then, the more I thought about it, it was going to cost me a car at some point. So I walked away from the deal satisfied."

Michael chimed in, "I hear you loud and clear. My day is coming, and I have to buy two cars!"

Robert continued, "The day I met Paige, I instantly felt this could become something special.

WHEN IT ALL FALLS APART

She is the type of woman I've imagined on my arm."
As he spoke, he looked into her eyes with a smooth-
ness that caused Jasmine to briefly envision Adrian
speaking of her in that manner. "Paige is sophisticated, beautiful inside and out. I find she's driven and
brutally honest to those she cares about."

Jasmine quickly blurted, "Yes, Lord! Amen,
brother! You're on it now! That's our Paige!"

Not to be upstaged, Paige replied, "Robert,
please don't get her started. She hates when I tell her
what she doesn't want to hear."

Jasmine popped Paige's leg, "Whatever!"

After a couple of hours of eating and laughing,
the evening came to a close. It was obvious there
were going to be more outings as a group. Michael
thought Robert was an upstanding guy. Likewise,
Robert felt he could learn a few things from Michael.
As they walked to the driveway, he didn't hesitate to
be honest with Michael.

"Hey, man, once again, I enjoyed myself.
Thanks for the invite. I was wondering if we could
get together and rap a little bit about a few things."

Michael was open for a little male bonding.
"No problem, my brother. Just let me know when.
What's up?"

Robert confessed, "Man, it's just. It's just that
I'm at the point where I want happiness. More than
having things, but real happiness. My impression of
you is that you are a man of faith. I admit I'm not
there yet. Trying to get there, but I'm not sure how to
actually get there, if you know what I mean. I know

199

I'm rambling, but going to church only reminds me how far behind I am spiritually. People seem to live a life I'm not living. I mean I'm not perfect, not by a long shot. Now, being with Paige, I see just how behind I am. I'm a prideful dude, so it's hard to say this, but I may be able to learn a few things from you, bro. I made a lot of mistakes with my ex-wife. Moving here and meeting Paige is my new beginning. I'm realizing I have to become something different."

Michael understood Robert and didn't hesitate to accept the mentoring role to help his fellow brother. "Man, I get where you are coming from and I'm here for you. We will get together and chop it up, but one thing I will tell you now. Don't expect to be perfect as you try to become better. Before you hire me as a mentor or whatever, it's best you know up front I'm far from perfect."

Robert nodded, "And that's the reason I put my pride aside and came to you. I need to learn from an imperfect man who happened to get it right along the way. Because that's who I'm trying to be."

Michael laughed and pounded fists with Robert, "Well, it sounds like a plan, my brother! We will strengthen each other."

Michael had no idea how true his statement was.

Chapter 14

. . . Failing to Juggle

Jasmine felt it was necessary to inform Adrian that Michael was home for good and it wasn't a good idea to continue their relationship. She apologized for the abrupt halt, but she had to refocus on her husband. Although Adrian felt used in a sense, he understood. He knew being involved with a married woman was shaky ground from the start. Out of desperation, he left the door open in case Jasmine ever needed him.

"Jasmine, the last thing I want is to become a problem for you. I knew this would happen eventually, but I admit I'm surprised it's ending this quickly. I realize the void in your life was temporary until your husband returned. For me, it's completely different. Going from relationship to relationship wasn't fulfilling anymore. Meeting you was refreshing. In your unique way, you challenged me. You caused me to open up in ways no other woman had before. And even though I knew you were married, it didn't stop my heart from connecting with you. I don't want to make this anymore difficult. I just want you to know I was drawn to you long before I touched you the way I did in my home."

Adrian had the ability to appeal to Jasmine in a way that caused her to ignore her intentions and pay more attention to his feelings. She began to feel guilty and somewhat obligated to help make his transition back into the world of dating as smooth as possible. Once again, she left a crack in the door. In efforts to wean him off of their affair, they talked occasionally during the workday. It was nothing like before. Most of the conversations were small talk. For Jasmine, it was like talking to a friend. On the other hand, it was a way for Adrian to feel connected to her. Each time they talked, Adrian fought back urges to tell Jasmine his feelings for her were progressing. Several weeks after Jasmine reset their relationship, Adrian decided to swim upstream and tell Jasmine exactly what he was feeling. He knew it could backfire, but it was worth a shot. Ironically, Jasmine wondered how she would feel when he began to date other women. A small part of her became saddened by the notion of his attention being given to someone else. Although she loved having Michael home, she began to notice her feelings for Adrian weren't dying as quickly as she imagined. One false move and she would find her-self performing a balancing act between both men. Michael was enjoying a well-deserved vacation after working tirelessly in California. He would make sure when Jasmine walked through the door after work, the house was spotless and dinner was prepared. He enjoyed being home and spending quality time with her. Nights watching their favorite television shows and sharing a bottle of Moscato were like an evening in paradise. To the naked eye, it seemed Jasmine had completely abandoned the Adrian saga as the Fletchers continued to double-date with Paige and Robert. A couple of weeks passed without any real communication. It was more of phone tag and brief voice mails. Despite her sporadic daydreaming, Jasmine's strategy to get over Adrian appeared to be working. However, her plan hit a snag when he decided to pay her a friendly visit. Adrian didn't know if she would be in meetings or anything, so he went to her job as the building opened and waited in the lobby. He hoped to catch her going to her office. Like clockwork, Jasmine appeared with coffee in one hand and her briefcase in another, power walking to the elevators. Adrian hopped to his feet and met her before she pressed the button to go up. "Ma'am, allow me."

Jasmine was surprised to see Adrian. "Hey, you! What are you doing here?"

Adrian smiled, "Well, since I was in the neighborhood, I thought I would stop by and tell you good morning face to face. You know, since we haven't really talked lately."

Jasmine gave him the *yeah, right* look. Reading her posture, he cut to the chase. "Well, I also stopped by to ask if we could have a sit down. There's something I need to talk to you about."

Jasmine looked somewhat concerned. "OK, is everything all right?"

Adrian replied, "No, no. Everything's good. I just need to come clean about some things."

Feeling she needed to allow him to get things off his chest, she invited him up. "Well, I have a little time before my first meeting. Let's talk in my office."

Once inside, Adrian looked around, pacing the floor making small talk, while Jasmine sat at her desk and logged into her computer. Eventually, he stopped and looked out onto Houston's downtown skyline and threw caution to the wind.

"Jasmine, I will try and be quick. I know we've talked about being friends and your husband being home; but honestly, it's been hard coping with the new arrangement. I've wrestled with telling you how I'm feeling for the last couple of weeks out of respect for your situation. I…I'm just going to get it over with. I don't know what will happen after I say this, but it's best I let you know."

Adrian turned away from the window and walked toward Jasmine. He stood on the other side of her desk and looked directly into her eyes.

"I know you are a married woman, but I'm in love with you!"

Mixed emotions shot through Jasmine like electricity. Part of her didn't feel like dealing with this revelation while her flesh delighted in this breaking news. Like a thrill seeker, Jasmine briefly contemplated getting back on the rollercoaster with Adrian.

However, she tried to avoid giving him the response he hoped for.

"Adrian, honestly, I don't know how to respond to that. I didn't expect this. I mean, I thought we…"

Before she finished her sentence Adrian interrupted, "Look, maybe this was a mistake. I'm only complicating your life."

As he walked toward the door, Jasmine stopped him. "Adrian, wait. Look, I just need some time to process all of this. We'll talk."

Adrian nodded his head as he slowly walked out. He left their meeting hopeful, while Jasmine sat feeling stuck between a rock and a hard place. Looking out of her window, she managed a smirk and verbalized, "What a hell of a way to start my day!" Needless to say, the following days were mentally taxing on Jasmine. Once again, Adrian found a way to stay alive in her heart. Temptation to keep him in her life became overwhelming. If she decided to keep Adrian around, it would require her to become a juggler of epic proportions. The more she thought of entering the next level of an adulterous lifestyle, the more questions popped into her head. For starters, will Adrian abide by the rules of the relationship? How would she restructure her routine at home? How many days a week would she see Adrian? Would she be able to handle sleeping with two men? More importantly, how will she be able to continue to look Michael in his loving eyes and pretend to be righteous? Finally, the million-dollar question surfaced. Is Adrian worth her marriage? Unfortunately, she wasn't able to answer those questions. Holding true to form, Satan caused a well-placed redirection. As she sat in her office, her colleague stuck his head in the door. "Hey, come on. They are waiting for us in the conference room."

Sadly, it wasn't long before Jasmine reverted back to an adulterous life. Satan's plot continued, and Phase 2 was in full affect. She seemed to had found a functional routine. Adrian thrived within his parameters and Michael didn't suspect anything in Jasmine's subtle adjustments. Every day that passed without incident created a stronger confidence in her deceitful strategy. Initially, she struggled on the days she slept with Adrian. Transforming mentally before walking into her home was difficult. However, the more she practiced, the better she got. The one thing she couldn't seem to overcome was the occasional mental visions of Michael while sleeping with Adrian and vice versa. Her sexual scheduling was pleasing to both men. Adrian adapted to intercourse once a week. Likewise, Michael unknowingly was also a team player with the frequency of intimacy. However, a glitch in the system came when the ladies decided to take the day off and do a little shopping. Paige waited in the car as Jasmine went to use the ATM machine. Jasmine's phone lit up as several text messages came through in succession. The constant dinging tempted Paige to take a peek at who was sending the messages. It wasn't out of the ordinary for Paige and Jasmine to answer each other's phone, so she didn't feel she was being nosey. The first line of the text appeared and Paige realized who the sender was. Jasmine returned to the car and noticed she had several text messages. Upon sight, she knew who it was and opted to read them later. Paige noticed her attempt to ignore the texts and took advantage of the chance to get a little clarity.

"So who is that blowing up your phone?"

Jasmine tried to downplay it, "Girl, I don't know. I'm trying to enjoy our day. If it was important, whoever it is would have called."

Paige replied, "So we're gonna act like that wasn't Adrian?"

Again, Jasmine tried to play it off. "Adrian? Now what makes you think out of all people it is Adrian?"

Paige sarcastically answered, "Well, 'cause I don't know why Michael would text how he wishes he could see you tonight. I don't know if it's Adrian or another man, but I do know it's not Michael."

Jasmine instantly became frustrated, "Paige, not now. It's not what you think. Don't mess up our day."

"Well, why don't you tell me what it is? 'Cause obviously, I was wrong for thinking you were done with that man."

Jasmine didn't anticipate on her day being filled with a confessional to Paige. She decided to give her a little info to cool her suspicion. "Like I said, it's not what you think. I told him Michael was home and I couldn't continue on like we were. He understood and we left it at that. We talk every once in a while, but it's nothing to be alarmed about."

Paige probed deeper, "So him saying he wishes he could see you tonight doesn't sound like an alarm? Then, I'm wondering, what doors have you left open to make him feel it's OK to say that to you?"

"Paige, relax. I have this under control."

"No, you don't have it under control. Looks like you are playing with fire to me."

Paige had a tendency to struggle with her tone. Jasmine began to take exception and became defensive.

"Look, I'm not in the mood for any of your damn sermons! I asked you to leave it alone and not screw up my day. You are really pushing it."

Paige replied, "I don't like how you are trying to act as if you are not doing anything wrong. Clearly, you already slept with him!"

"First of all, who are you to assume I've opened my legs for any man other than my husband? Secondly, I don't like your tone and how you are in my business. If I don't ask for your opinion, keep it to yourself!"

Things went south very quickly. Usually, Jasmine could handle Paige's delivery, but things were different now. She had become protective of her affair and wasn't afraid to alienate herself from her best friend. Without warning, she turned the car around to take Paige back home. Paige lost her composure and began to shout, "You kept things away from me because you knew I wasn't going to agree with you! You know what you're doing is jacked up! That's probably why you were always suggesting we go on double dates. You had the audacity to not only use Robert and I, but you used your husband to fight your temptations. You didn't cling to Michael once he came home out of pure love. You needed him to draw you away from Adrian, because you were too much of a coward to face the devil! Like I told you, this is what happens when you try to put a Band-Aid on a gunshot wound!"

Jasmine screamed, "Who in the hell do you think you are to tell me why I got closer to my damn husband? For the last time, mind your business!"

It was strange for them to be at odds. However, it was clear phase 2 of Satan's plan was working. Breaking Jasmine's connection to hear spiritual advice was a key component to her destruction. Silence filled the car until Jasmine stopped in front of Paige's home. Before getting out, Paige gave her closing remarks.

"To be clear, I don't apologize for saying you are messing up, girl! What are you going to do when it all falls apart?"

Paige got out of the car and slammed the door! Jasmine drove off while briefly imagining that horrific outcome.

Chapter 15

... God Isn't Pleased

———— ◆ ————

Michael's satisfaction of not having any projects to complete and deadlines to meet began to bore him. He was rested and wanted back in the game. He decided to call Tracy Sprewell for any opportunities. He was hoping there was a chance he could do some production work for other artists from Houston. Unfortunately, she didn't answer. He left a voice mail and figured she would call back when she got a chance. After doing so, he went to the gym to workout. During the drive, he began to think about Jasmine. For the first time, he questioned if she was preoccupied with something. He tried to understand their inconsistent sex life, assuming it was due to the increased demands of her job and being a full-time mom and wife. However, he didn't understand why things seemed to also take a hit, emotionally. She did less touching and showed less attention. It wasn't a drastic decline but enough to cause Michael to think about it for a moment. Because he didn't have anything concrete to base his concerns, he let those thoughts dissipate. Maybe his time off was causing his gages to be a bit off kilter. A couple of days later, Tracy Sprewell returned his call. She had better news than he could have imagined.

"Michael, how are you my friend? I heard your voice mail. I had to laugh because I was preparing to get in touch with you, so I could entice you with something."

Michael's head rose like a startled deer. "Well, let's hear it!"

"We have been planning to open a division in Houston for a while. It's been on the back burner for about a year. Now, they are ready to move forward. My bosses really loved what you did here. Everyone feels you would be the perfect guy to head our southern region. It would be a tremendous amount of work, but hopefully, your salary would motivate you."

"Tracy, are you serious? This is crazy! I was thinking producing tracks and you are talking major operations!"

She said, "Well, I believe it was you that told me His ways are not our ways and His thoughts are not our thoughts. Plus, this could be a two-way blessing, 'cause if you decline, they are prepared to send me and a sister ain't trying to leave California. And yes, I said ain't! So I need you more than they do!"

"Well, all I can say is God has answered your prayers, 'cause I want the job!"

Tracy replied, "I will be in touch with more details. I do know we are in the process of finding a location there in Houston. We looked at a few spots and have one in mind. I'm anticipating on coming out there and meet with the seller when we decide to make a move. I want you to join in on that meeting when I do. In the meantime, we will put together a formal offer for you so you can sign on the dotted line, sir."

"Sounds good to me! I'll be waiting." After hanging up, Michael paused to thank God. The decision to go to California proved to be a life-changing move. He shouted, "Lord, you truly know how to put things together for those who love you! Thank you!" It was going to be hard to keep it to himself, but he wanted to wait and surprise Jasmine. The following weeks were challenging for him. He almost let the cat out of the bag several times.

Ironically, Adrian was experiencing similar opportunity. A business proposal fell into his lap that would cause his portfolio to skyrocket. Likewise, he couldn't wait to tell Jasmine. For both men, she was the queen of their eye. Adrian wanted the deal to materialize before he broke the news to her. He owned property throughout the city. One particular building sat dormant for years. Many times, he thought of taking a loss and sell the unprofitable real estate. His mother always talked him off of the ledge, claiming one day the right deal would come. He stood on that very property with tears in his eyes, wishing she were alive to witness what was about to happen. A smile replaced his tears when he thought of Jasmine and how she would be a lovely stand in for his mother. Jasmine noticed how both of them seemed jovial. Her double life became easier as a result. Having become self-indulging, she assumed they were happy because she was doing an excellent job pleasing the both of them. Adrian couldn't hold it in. While talking to Jasmine, he decided to hint around his lucrative opportunity.

"Babe, life is good! I mean things seem to be working in my favor. I'm in a good place with you and business is great. I really like my position right now. Then again, I know one other thing that could happen to put me over the top, but I won't go there."

Adrian took a sidebar to hint around having Jasmine as his own would ensure ultimate happiness. He continued, "I've been sitting on some news I want to share with you. I don't want to jinx it, so I'll give you just a taste. I've been sitting on some property for a while. The only thing that kept me from selling it was the words my mother spoke over it. Now, I'm glad I did, because it looks like it may bring in a gigantic profit. I don't have any specifics right now, but I was hoping when the time comes to meet, you would join me and be a second ear."

Jasmine showed excitement for Adrian's opportunity and agreed to join him. "Sure, I don't see why not. I would just need to know in advance so I could clear my schedule."

Adrian replied, "I have a question. If I wanted to use your company for a project and let's say you actually brokered the deal, would you get a commission?"

Jasmine answered while trying to figure out his angle. "Yes, I would, sir. Why?"

"Well, if this deal goes through, I want to develop another piece of property I have my eyes on and who better to get my business than you. It would be my way of sewing into your career. The more I build, the more you profit."

Jasmine liked the sound of that, but she had a very important question. "That sounds like a master plan, but how much of that is contingent on our current arrangement?"

Adrian quickly deflected, "None of it. Business is business. You don't get to this level of success by being emotional. If I make money, you make money regardless of our status. Believe that!"

Weeks went by and Michael held strong and didn't give Jasmine a single detail of what was on the horizon. The call Michael anticipated finally came. Tracy informed him she would be in Houston within a week to meet with the seller. She also reminded Michael that she wanted him to accompany her to the meeting.

"Last but not the least, your contract is ready to be signed. I'm sure you'll be more than pleased. I was thinking we could take care of it prior to our meeting."

Michael was overjoyed and looked forward to his workweek! He wanted to celebrate although he wasn't ready to reveal anything just yet. He told the boys to dress up in their black suits as he prepared a very special dinner. The table was decorated with candles and what Jasmine referred to as her good plates and glasses. He called Jasmine and told her to let him know when she was on her way home. After going out to grab a dozen of roses, he gave a few instructions to the boys. By the time Jasmine pulled up, Brandon was standing on the curb at the end of the driveway. As Jasmine slowed down, he walked to the driver's side door.

"Good evening, ma'am."

Jasmine had a puzzled look on her face. "Brandon, what are you doing, boy?"

He ignored her question and stuck to the script. He handed her a slip of paper with valet written on it. "You look lovely tonight. Welcome to Fletcher's. Enjoy your evening!" He grabbed her hand to help her out of the car. While Brandon parked the car, Chris met Jasmine halfway up the driveway to escort her to her table. The formal dining room resembled an actual restaurant. The boys helped Michael bring all the fixings to the table. It looked more like Thanksgiving by the time they were done. Jasmine didn't understand why the Fletcher men went to great lengths.

"Well, needless to say, I'm very impressed! My babies are looking handsome and my husband is sweeping me off my feet. Fletch, you are the man!"

Michael had a suave look on his face and replied, "Girl, this is only the tip of the iceberg. You truly haven't seen nothing yet!"

Jasmine blushed, "Michael don't get me riled up in front these boys! We will have to skip this dinner if you keep this up."

Chris quickly interrupted, "Hey, can we eat please? I didn't get dressed up for all of that."

They all laughed and enjoyed a beautiful family dinner. Days passed and the night before Tracy was due to land in Houston, Michael was struggling to hold it together. Jasmine knew she would be home late the next day, so she wanted to make sure Michael knew.

"Oh, before I forget. I am working a little late tomorrow. I didn't know if you had any plans for us."

Michael didn't know how long the meeting with Tracy would last, so it was actually good for the both of them. "That's cool, sweetheart. I have some running around to do anyway. Maybe we can meet up for dinner somewhere."

Jasmine agreed before lying down for the night. As the sun beamed through their bedroom window, Michael sat on the edge of the bed thanking God in advance for what was about to happen. Jasmine went to work earlier than usual. She had to finish a few things before leaving at noon. It was the day Adrian asked her to join him at his business meeting. When he called with the address and time of the meeting, Jasmine assured him she would be there. Before hanging up, she asked him a quick question. "Hey, do you have a real estate agent working your deal?"

Adrian replied, "Well, you're talking to him. I try to cut out the middleman as much as possible. Now that I think about it, that probably explains why it has taken this long to sell the property. So it will be just us two today!"

When Tracy and her assistant landed, she had her call Michael to let him know a car would be there to pick him up. "Hello, Michael? This is Ms. Sprewell's assistant Amanda Taylor. I…"

Michael anxiously interrupted, "Amanda, how are you?"

"I'm doing great. Ms. Sprewell wanted me to inform you that your ride should be there soon. I also would like to give you an idea of our schedule today. The driver is going to bring you to our hotel. We reserved a conference room, where we will hopefully finalize your contract and show you the proposed layout for the new division. After doing so, we will go to lunch and prepare to meet with the seller."

Michael seemed game ready. "Sounds like a plan! I look forward to seeing you two again." As he waited for his ride, tears filled his eyes. He was about to enter the next level!

It wasn't long before there was a knock at the door. Michael's chariot had arrived and he headed off to the hotel. By the time the car stopped, his hands were sweaty. Tracy and Amanda sat in the lounge area waiting for him. "Michael, over here!" They exchanged pleasantries and headed to the conference room. Once inside they did a little catching up before getting down to business. Tracy slid Michael's contract over to him. Michael immediately saw the figure and leaned back in his chair with his mouth completely open. With all professional composure out of the window, he managed to utter, "Are you freaking kidding me?" The offer far superseded his expectations. Tracy and Amanda looked at each other and then turned to Michael.

Tracy jokingly added, "I knew it wasn't enough."

Michael rubbed his chin and smiled, "Yeah, right! Give me that pen!" As he signed, his emotions were flying high. "My wife is going to faint! This is crazy!" It was easy to see his humility. He always believed in his abilities; however, he obviously underestimated the X factor he possessed. The rest of the morning was used to go over the layout and some expectations for the new division. Tracy finished her spill and felt it was time to grab a bite to eat.

"Well, that's about all I have right now. How about we head to lunch?"

Michael and Amanda agreed. "Amanda, can you have valet bring the car? I'll meet you both up front in a sec. I want to call the seller and reconfirm our start time."

Tracy proceeded to make her call and afterwards headed to the car.

While Michael was preoccupied with the ladies, Jasmine had trouble getting out of the office early. An unscheduled conference call took priority. She called to let Adrian know.

"Hey, I have a little bad news."

Adrian instantly thought she was pulling out of the meeting. "Please don't tell me you changed your mind!"

Jasmine replied, "Hold on, let me finish. I just found out we have a conference call in thirty minutes. All of the higher-ups are in on this one. There is no way I can duck out early. As soon as it's over, I will call you and see where you are. Don't worry; I will be there for the meeting. I may be running a little behind though."

Adrian took a sigh of relief, "Oh, that's better than what I was thinking. As long as you can get there, I'm good."

Once the trio finished their power lunch, they began their journey to meet the seller and walk the property. While riding, Michael asked, "Tracy, what are the chances of sealing the deal today?"

"Well, I believe we have a tentative deal ready to go. A lot of things were done prior to me coming today. It's basically a matter of walking the property, liking what we see and giving the OK to have our construction guys come and strategize for remodeling. I feel extremely confident it will be finalized today."

Soon thereafter, they arrived on site. Michael liked the presentation of the building from the onset. "So far, so good." Amanda nodded in agreement. Tracy made a call to notify the seller they were there. As they walked in, Tracy began pointing and referring to the layout she brought with her. With their back to the rear of the building, the seller appeared.

"Well hello, I'm glad you all made it. I'm Adrian Moore. Which one of you beautiful ladies is Ms. Sprewell?"

Tracy reached out her hand to formally greet Adrian. "Hello, Mr. Moore. I'm Ms. Sprewell, but please call me Tracy. It's nice to finally put a face with the voice from our phone conversations. This is my assistant Amanda and the head man of our new division, Michael."

Adrian had no idea who Michael was. He didn't make any connections. At that point, he was in full business mode. He greeted Michael with a handshake and friendly pat on the shoulder.

"How are you doing, Michael? Man, you're a tall guy! I really hope you all like the building. In my opinion, it has a certain elegance throughout."

Looking around, they all agreed. Twenty minutes into the tour, Adrian realized he missed Jasmine's text. After reading it, he decided to call her back.

"Please pardon me for one moment. I forgot to mention we will be joined by my assistant and she's running a little behind."

The trio excused Adrian as he stepped aside to call Jasmine. "Hey, I got your text. How far away are you?"

Jasmine replied, "I'll be there in five minutes."

Adrian wanted Jasmine to see him in action. He couldn't wait until she got there. "OK, sweetheart. When you get here, come to the fourth floor and turn left after you go through the double doors."

Neither the Fletchers nor Adrian knew of the collision that was about to take place. Minutes later, the bell from the elevator rang. Jasmine stepped out and walked through the double doors. Her head was angled down as she was in the process of putting her sunglasses in her purse. Simultaneously, Adrian began to introduce his assistant. "All right, here she is! Ladies and gentleman, this is my assistant and girl-friend, Jasmine Fletcher."

Jasmine lifted her head to greet them and locked eyes with her loving husband! Tracy was completely dazed, having met Jasmine in California. The feelings that shot through Michael were paralyzing! Time seemed to freeze in the midst of complete chaos! During the deafening silence, Jasmine began to lose all faculties. Her physical body was upright in comparison to her emotions and spirit being shattered on the floor like tiny shards of glass. Questions from every angle filled her brain. "What is Michael doing here? Isn't that the lady he worked for in California? Is my marriage over? What have I done?"

Thoughts of all the loving efforts of her husband stabbed her heart, sounds of her boys' laughter seemed to morph into demonic giggling, and finally, the words spoken by her caring friend blared in her ears, "What are you going to do when it all falls apart?"

To the naked eye, Michael seemed stoic. As time stood still, he quickly thought of what he could lose if he overreacted. He read numerous times about being slow to anger in the Bible. This moment seemed like the ultimate final exam to graduate to God's next level for his life. He felt he had to suppress the havoc Jasmine wreaked on his heart for the sake of his opportunity. It seemed as if the Holy Spirit whispered, "Not now. Not here. Finish this deal." Michael had to think quickly, realizing at that moment, Satan was trying to steal his wife and blessing all at once. Time resumed and Michael extended his hand to Jasmine. "Nice to meet you, I'm Michael." Jasmine and Tracy couldn't believe his impromptu. It was somewhat scary to watch a man go unfazed by his wife being introduced as another man's girlfriend. It literally caused Jasmine to fear being alone with her husband. After seeing his response, she found an awkward sense of security with the others around. Surprisingly, the tour continued. Michael was a silent partner as he walked along nodding in agreement to statements made by Tracy and Adrian. Tracy knew to intercept any questions Adrian directed to Michael. As she feared, a question was thrown his way.

"Tell me, Michael, what corner would you like for your office? The right side of the floor has a beautiful view of Allen Parkway."

Jasmine saw her husband's reluctance to respond. Just before Adrian could sense a problem, Tracy interjected, "In that case, I would take that one. I will be in town periodically and that sounds like a replica of my office in California."

Everyone laughed with the exception of Michael, as he stood behind Adrian. By the time the meeting came to a close, Tracy gave the final OK. Jasmine knew staying back or walking out with Adrian was not a smart move. She pretended to get an important text to excuse herself. Before walking out, Michael watched as Adrian gently grabbed Jasmine's hand in concern of her leaving prematurely.

"Is everything OK?"

Jasmine's eyes were beginning to water and turn red. She said softly, "I have an emergency at home. I have to go."

As everything unfolded before Ms. Sprewell, she saw another innate ability Michael possessed. Although she was saddened for her friend and colleague, she admired his resolve to remain cool in the saddle. She wanted to talk to him immediately after the meeting, but she didn't want her assistant to hear the conversation. Amanda didn't have any idea what happened, but she sensed something was wrong. She thought the ride back to the hotel was going to be a joyful journey. On the contrary, it was more like a ride to a funeral. Once they arrived, Tracy gave Ms. Taylor a trivial task to allow her to talk to Michael.

He tried to finish the afternoon as professional as possible, although he was not only hurt but also embarrassed.

"Well, Tracy, you did it! Look, I don't want you to worry about my situation and if I'll be able to do the job. I won't let anything stop me from being the best I can be."

Tracy looked at him with empathy and replied, "Michael, I'm so sorry you have to go through this. I do know you have what it takes to bounce back. While in California, you encouraged so many people; but sometimes, the one who encourages need to be encouraged. Listen to me! People saw the compassion in you. Today, I saw you apply the word of God in a situation most men would have abandoned and completely flipped. You have to know God is pleased with you. I know right now this doesn't ease your pain, but there is favor on your life and this storm will pass! You are being tested. I witnessed a man react slowly to get God's promise. You have to know the promise isn't just ensuring you move forward in your job. The promise is He will never leave you or forsake you. I believe your marriage will be restored because of that promise."

Michael knew Tracy was speaking the absolute truth, and he appreciated her effort. However, it didn't have much effect on the hole in his heart. He thanked her and asked for her continued prayers. She ended the conversation by letting him know they planned to remain in Houston for a couple of days to finalize paperwork on the building in case he needed them for anything. As he walked to the awaiting car to take him home, he received a text message from Jasmine.

Chapter 16

. . . The Aftermath

Jasmine felt Michael's handling of such a heart-breaking revelation was as misleading as standing in the eye of a hurricane. The storm was far from over. She envisioned total chaos and became afraid to go home. Her first inclination was to call Paige and ask to stay the night. However, that thought quickly disappeared as she remembered their last conversation. Instead, she opted to get a hotel room. Before going into the hotel lobby, she realized the last thing she wanted was Michael to think she was with Adrian. Therefore, she sent Michael a text and informed him of her plans. She didn't know if he would come to the hotel and blow up, but she was out of options at that point. For the first time, Jasmine was afraid Michael would hit her. In many regards, she felt she deserved nothing less. The look on his face destroyed her on the inside. All she could repeat in her head is she have just lost the best husband in the world! He is going to leave and there's nothing she could do to change it. The mere thought caused her to helplessly fall unto the steering wheel of her car and let out a thunderous scream! She sat nervously awaiting a response. Minutes later, the phone began to ring. The screen lit up displaying the words, *My Man*. It was Michael calling and her anxiety level instantly rose to an all-time high! She answered the phone with a frightened voice. "Hel-Hello." There was silence for five eerie seconds. As Jasmine's heart seemed to stop beating, Michael's voice began to pierce her spirit like a spear.

"Why in the hell did you do this to me? All I ever tried to do was make you and our children happy! The day I'm excited to share some great news, I find out my wife has a boyfriend! You can forget about going to a damn hotel! We need to talk!"

Jasmine sat speechless, as her heart trembled. She slowly closed her eyes as tears fell one by one like a steady drip from a leaky faucet. Michael continued and gave her an ultimatum.

"If you are not at home before I get there, just keep driving!"

After his demand, he hung up. Jasmine knew she had to go home and face the consequences. She felt the children should not be in the house to witness their parents do and say things they were not accustomed to. If her boys heard the things she had done, she would die. She decided to have them go to a friend's house for the night. An hour later, Jasmine heard the front door opening. Her hands began to shake. Michael walked in with a defeated look on his face. He looked as if street punks roughed him up in the back alley. His tie was loosely draped around his neck, his shirt was untucked, and his eyes were weak. Everything about his appearance suggested he had hit rock bottom. The sight of her husband caused her to place both hands over her mouth as the slow drip of tears picked up pace. Michael sat lifeless on the sofa and said nothing. Again, there was awkward silence between them. Jasmine broke the silence and began talking.

"Michael, baby, I…"

The second Michael heard the word *baby*, he pointed at her with fire in his eyes and shouted to the top of his lungs, "Don't call me that! Don't call me baby! Say what you have to say, but don't refer to me as your baby!" He then became silent once again, allowing Jasmine to continue.

"Michael, I have no excuse for what I allowed myself to be a part of. I was selfish and you did nothing to deserve this. I know I deserve whatever happens to us. I'm ashamed and so sorry for what I've done. I can't imagine the shock of seeing me there with another man. Please believe me, I am not his girlfriend! I'm lost for words at this point and I know saying I'm sorry won't undo anything."

Michael never lifted his head as Jasmine spoke. It was like he was in a comatose state. Without looking at her, through gritted teeth, he finally spoke. "Today was supposed to be the beginning of new blessings for me and my family. You have completely flipped our world upside down! Who in the hell are you?"

Jasmine desperately answered, "I'm your wife!"

Michael returned, "And you are also his girl-friend! It's clear his feelings for you goes beyond sex. Who is this man and, again, why in the hell did you do this to me? Damn it, I want the truth!"

Jasmine knew she couldn't sugarcoat anything. The hardest thing to do was look her husband in the eyes and explain how she allowed another man to lure her and enter into her essence. She thought of placing majority of the blame on Adrian. However, she realized the last thing she needed to do was appear helpless in another man's web. Jasmine knew the real truth is her attraction to Adrian and curiosity of his mystique was a turn on for her. If she wanted her marriage, it was time to reveal some things about herself Michael wasn't aware of. A quick vision of Paige popped in her mind.

"Jas, trust God will save your marriage. You must tell him everything. Expose what you've become, so the healing process can begin for the both of you."

Although filled with fear, she began. "I don't really know where to start. I met him after you left for Los Angeles. We were not in pursuit of each other when we first met. I mean, he seemed nice and became just another person to talk to from time to time like associates. I didn't think anything of it because I wasn't looking to mess around. Over time, we began to talk more and things just got out of hand."

When she actually began talking, she abandoned the mission to tell her husband everything in detail. Jasmine hoped the short uneventful version was good enough. However, Michael wasn't that easy to satisfy.

"Things got of hand?" Michael quickly went to the ultimate question. "Jasmine, how many times did you open your legs?"

She quickly answered, "Michael, I never slept with that man. I admit I...I kissed him but I never slept with him!"

As truthful as Jasmine wanted to be, she refused to tell her husband she willingly had sex with Adrian. Michael's demeanor changed drastically as he slapped a bottle of water off of the table.

"Jasmine, I was a thousand miles away for months. You got involved with a man, kissed him, met him for a business meeting to be a trophy piece, and got introduced as his girlfriend; and you sit here and feed me this bullsh...!"

Before he could finish his sentence, Jasmine screamed, "Michael, I'm sorry! Lord, help me! Michael, please believe me!"

At this point, Michael was losing his patience with his wife. He pounded his right fist into his left hand and yelled, "Jasmine, save the damn theatrics! You can't sweep this under the rug. Again, woman, I want the truth!"

Fearing her evasive tactics would only cause more problems, she decided to give Michael a sample size of the truth. There was no way she was going to reveal the actual number of sexual sessions she had with Adrian. "Just once! Just once, Michael! I was wrong! I'm so sorry!"

Jasmine's face was covered with tears. Her eyes were blood shot red. Her face appeared to droop in despair. She had just admitted to having sex with another man to her loving husband! Jasmine felt she was having an out of body experience. He knew the truth already, but hearing her say it shot through his heart like a bullet. He quickly realized he wasn't prepared for such a confirmation. It literally dropped him to his knees! It was a classic example of the old cliché, "Be careful what you ask for." The sounds of heartache that Michael bellowed was evidence his world had shattered. Jasmine joined him on the floor, pleading for his forgiveness, trying her best to reassure him that she loves him. The scene in the Fletcher's home was disheartening to say the least. Their marriage had suddenly suffered a disastrous blow. Michael cried intensely while repeating, "Why? Why, Jasmine? Why did you do this? Why?" Obviously, her interrogation was not over. Her attempt to give a generic explanation was a waste of time. She had no choice but to tell him everything if she wanted a chance to save her marriage. Mentally, she prepared to lie on the altar and offer herself for sacrifice. Her voice became more absolute, yet compassionate and apologetic.

"OK, Michael, here is the truth. Promise me you will keep it together while I explain." With watery eyes, Michael agreed to keep his composure. Jasmine continued, "Please understand what I've done has nothing to do with the type of man you are and what you've been as a husband in this marriage.

You have been what most women pray for. I lost my way because I got caught up. Adrian presented a different experience. His world isn't as routine and regimented. While you were gone, as a woman, I longed for companionship. It got to a point phone conversations between you and I weren't enough. I wanted to sit and look into your eyes, lay with you, and be touched. I should have told you how I was feeling, but I thought it would be selfish of me to add more pressure on you. I would listen to the fatigue in your voice from working countless hours. I understood you were trying to do your best and your mind needed to be clear. Therefore, I didn't want to put any extra burden on you. However, I was getting lonely. Obviously, Adrian isn't you, but I somehow settled for a substitute. Although I know and love the Lord, I got weak. To be honest, I've learned a lot about who I am through all of this. I regret the damage it has done, but I see I'm not as spiritually strong as I imagined. I now see how much I depended on you for my spiritual walk. Michael, you have always been the spiritual backbone for this family. When I was tired from the stress of my career, you were there to remind me of God's word and encourage me to trust Him. I didn't have to tell you. You just knew when I needed encouragement. By you being in California, there was no way of you knowing I was on the spiritual decline and my flesh was getting weak for your touch."

Michael broke his promise to remain composed and yelled, "Jasmine, don't give me that! We both make money! You could have come to California every other weekend if you needed my touch. If you really wanted me, I would have come to you. Your weakness had nothing to do with me. It was for that man! You think I'm stupid?"

For the first time in his marriage, Michael wanted to physically harm his wife. Before he gave way to his evil intentions, he felt it would be best to get out of there. He stood up and grabbed his keys off of the bar. Jasmine grabbed his hand and begged him not to leave. She promised to tell him the truth about Adrian. It was extremely hard to tell Michael her darkest secrets. However, she gathered herself, wiped the tears from her eyes, and pressed on.

"Adrian's world appealed to another side of me and it drew me away from my spirituality. I mean as a woman, I was intrigued by the romance and seduction. I allowed myself to be drawn to the unknown he presented. Michael, I wrestled with the fact that he was not my husband and I was going down the wrong path. I pushed away and tried to refocus. However, I'm ashamed to admit the struggle to stay away became a slugfest between my spirit and flesh. The night we...we had...you know; I was trying to be a friend. His mother had died and he had been drinking. He asked me to come to his home because his mom lived with him and he would have a hard time being there. Michael, I know this isn't a consolation, but my intention wasn't to sleep with him. Once I got there, somehow, I allowed myself to be seduced. One thing led to another, and unfortunately, it happened. I thought when you came home things would go back to normal. My life would resume. My focus would be redirected. I told him we couldn't continue seeing each other. I felt this was something that would eventually fade away because my focus was back on you. Then, I realized it wasn't that easy. My flesh wouldn't surrender. I found myself loving you but also wanting to be around Adrian. I knew I had to stop, but spiritually, I didn't have the strength to fight off the desires to juggle two relationships. Now that everything has happened, I'm dying inside because there's no question who I truly want!"

While she explained, Michael began to second-guess going to Los Angeles. He felt the opportunity to get ahead wasn't worth the sanctity of his marriage. Jasmine paused and stared at Michael with a sincere face. She waited for an indication of what was going through his head. He looked at her as composed as he could manage and replied. "Jasmine, things may be clear to you now because light has entered into your dark convenient world. What snake is comfortable living its life in plain view? You say you want me. But maybe it's because you were put in a position that forced you to choose. And that's the problem right there. If you had to be forced, are you sure choosing me is what you really want? You could have made that choice the day I came home. Honestly, I don't think you've given this enough time to actually know what you want. I am certain you love me. However, I'm not certain you didn't fall in love with that dude."

Jasmine abruptly interjected, "Michael, I don't love him! I don't know enough about him to love him."

Michael gave a sarcastic grin and returned fire, "Wow, I don't know what's worse, my wife having sex with a man before loving him or loving him before having sex. I guess both scenarios indicate I don't know you like I thought!" Michael decided they both needed some time apart. He stood up again and walked to the bedroom. Minutes later, he reappeared and walked toward the front door. Before walking out, he turned around and said, "And another damn thing, I know you had sex more than once! We both know the truth!" Jasmine didn't respond. This time, she lowered her head in disgust. The pain in his voice hit her harder than any physical punch he could have delivered. He continued, "I'm going to a hotel for a couple of days. We both have a lot of things to think about. I don't feel a quick decision will be a solid decision for this marriage."

Jasmine didn't want him to leave. She didn't feel her decision was premature. She knew exactly who she wanted. However, she understood Michael needed some time. All she could do was let him go and pray he'll decide to forgive her and give her another chance. As he walked out of the front door with a backpack of clothes and essentials, Jasmine softly said, "I love you."

Without turning around, he waved his right hand in efforts to say, "Yeah, whatever!" She became physically sick from heartache, as she watched him drive away.

Chapter 17

... Critical Condition

Michael sat in the hotel room replaying everything in his mind. He thought he knew the woman he married. He felt they were inseparable. Her actions destroyed his comfort zone he found in his marriage. He was filled with heartache and regret. Had he known Jasmine was a flight risk, he wouldn't have gone to California. Michael kept mulling over what he could have missed. What did he do wrong? Why didn't he come home periodically? Was he overbearing with his do right approach to life? Was his wife bored with him? The more he wrecked his brain for an explanation, the more it became apparent this was out of his hands. He was blindsided by his wife, his friend, his everything. He didn't believe in questioning God, but this was too much. Staring into the bathroom mirror, he asked, "What was the purpose for this? Why are you letting this happen?" He waited for an answer that he didn't get. God's voice didn't resound and satisfy his curiosity. Michael was left to deal with silence. Eventually, the physical and emotional exhaustion took toll on his body. Pain and confusion finally rocked him to sleep.

On the contrary, Jasmine couldn't sleep, nor did she want too. Several phone calls to Michael went straight to voice mail. She was at the point of desperation. Ironically, Paige called. She hadn't talked to her friend since the day they had a falling out over Adrian. Jasmine looked at the phone wondering, "Why is she calling me? Did Michael tell her what happened? Should I answer? Is it time to hear what I don't want to hear?" Although Jasmine wasn't in the mood for Paige's *I told you so* speech, she decided to pick up. She sounded like the old Paige when Jasmine answered. "Well, hello stranger! I was wondering if you still loved me."

Jasmine replied with skepticism, "Girl, you know better than that." Jasmine felt the real questions were coming.

Paige sensed a little dryness in her friend and asked, "Did I catch you at a bad time?"

Jasmine returned, "No, why do you ask?"

"You seem preoccupied. Are you OK?"

Dealing with a heavy heart, Jasmine quickly became irritated with Paige's bait and hook approach and decided to bypass the setup questions. "Paige, why did you really call? What did you hear?"

She was thrown by Jasmine's questions. "What I heard? What are you talking about?"

Her friend sounded genuinely confused. Feeling she may have misread her motive, she tried to camouflage her suspicions. "I'm sorry, I thought you were about to continue our last conversation."

Paige responded, "No, I called to open the line of communication again. Bringing up Adrian would only put a bigger wedge between us. I'm sure there will be a time and place for that conversation."

Jasmine privately thought, "The time couldn't be anymore perfect than right now." Again, questions exploded like bombs in her mind. "Should I tell her? Can she help me with Michael? Is this God sending refuge? Will she tear me down for this?" Mentally, Jasmine was all over the place. Suddenly, for the first time since the catastrophe, she heard a divine voice. "Sometimes, correction is painful, but necessary. Tell her everything." Jasmine obeyed what she heard and told Paige everything from start to finish. Crying throughout, she managed to expose the passion she had for Adrian and how Michael found out. Surprisingly, Paige listened without interruption, understanding the role she played in this moment was crucial. Once Jasmine emptied her tank, Paige felt reassurance was all she needed at the time.

"First of all, I hate this has happened. Both of you are family to me. I love you and I'm willing to do anything to help mend your marriage. But I want you to listen to me, your marriage isn't over. Michael just needs time. We will make it through this."

Jasmine felt a small amount of hope knowing Paige would help in the healing process. She even laughed a little as she spoke, "So no fire and brimstone? No, I told you so?"

Paige replied, "Oh, I keep me some fire and brimstone to burn your tail, but this isn't the time. Don't worry, our *come to Jesus* meeting is on the schedule."

Paige being Paige caused Jasmine to smile. She admitted to her best friend, "I'm so glad you called. You are truly my sister and I'm sorry I didn't listen. Thank you for being here for me."

Paige knew her friend loved her husband. Her heart truly went out to her. "Sweetie, we will get through this. I'm not leaving your side."

The next morning, Michael was still dazed. He wanted to vent, but he didn't have anyone to talk to. He didn't want to involve his family in his problems. Even though Jasmine hurt him deeply, he cared about how his parents would see her. They loved Jasmine, and until he knew his next course of action, he thought it would be best to keep them out of it. He had eight voice mails and eleven text messages waiting for him. Ten messages were from his wife and one strangely from Robert. Paige had begun phase1 of the healing process by recruiting Robert to reach out to Michael. He skimmed through the repetitive pleas from Jasmine and eventually got to Robert's message. It was a typical guylike text, saying he wanted to hook up and go somewhere to watch a few basketball games. Michael felt it was good timing. He needed to stay busy; therefore, he agreed, and they met hours later at a local sports bar.

Michael arrived first and grabbed a pub table. Robert walked in shortly thereafter and gave Michael a fist bump, "Big fella, it's been a minute. How have you been?"

Michael returned greetings, "What's happening? Just been busy man. I'm glad you hit me up. I needed to get out and chill."

Paige reminded Robert not to initiate anything. Let Michael talk. Although it would be a slim chance, they hoped he would open up. They wasted no time ordering an entire chicken coop of wings with all the fixings and talked sports for a while.

"I assume being from Chicago, you are a die-hard Bulls fan."

Robert laughed, "You already know! You can't be from Chi-town and go against the Bulls. Now, I do admit I root for LeBron no matter what team he plays for."

Michael echoed, "I feel you. But I'm ride or die with my Rockets!"

Robert replied, "Man, can you imagine the money these guys make nowadays? Jordan, Bird, and Magic were great…"

Michael interrupted, "And Olajuwon."

"My fault, sir. And Olajuwon were great, but the money was nowhere near what they are getting now. If I had a fourth of that money, my worries from here on out would be over."

That statement triggered Michael. He thought, "I disagree. Money means nothing when your joy and peace of mind is gone." He wanted to open up and tell Robert what had been thrown in his lap. Instantly, Satan laughed and actually encouraged him to do so.

"Go ahead and tell him. Let him know his spiritual mentor is weak and broken. This is going to be good! The teacher is seeking help from the student. This is like the blind leading the blind."

Michael almost fell for the devil's trick. For a second, he considered Satan's sarcasm. His pride almost got the best of him, as he processed, "I don't really know this dude. He asked to me to help him spiritually. How can he possibly help me? Keep people out of your business. Be a man and deal with this alone."

Before he missed an opportunity, God spoke. Finally, there was the voice Michael had been waiting to hear. Anticipating an impactful word, he paused to listen. On the contrary, God was very brief. "Don't be foolish to think the teacher can't learn."

He knew what God meant. Expecting something was going to be said to help him, he decided to open up.

"Rob, I used to think if Jasmine and I had millions, life would be like a bed of roses. I don't see it that way anymore."

Rob replied, "Well, how would you know until you actually had that kind of money?"

Michael hesitated. He knew if he was going to explain his situation, he would have to reveal some things to a guy he barely knew. Throwing caution to the wind, he disclosed his personal info. "Well, that's not completely true. Yesterday, I accepted a job that will pay me one million dollars a year for the next six years. It also included a quarter of a million dollar signing bonus. I'm not in the league, but I'd say that pretty much makes me a baller. When I saw the figures, I almost fell out of my seat!"

Robert almost choked on a chicken bone when he heard the amount. "Hol...ho...hold on! You what?"

Michael continued, "Slow down, man. Don't choke while you are with me. I don't want my signing bonus paying off your lawsuit." They both laughed and Michael continued, "But seriously, man, my big blessing landed in my hands. Unfortunately, I couldn't enjoy it due to another surprise that made its way to me." Like his wife had done hours before, he gave Robert a detailed play-by-play account of the worst day of his life. By the time he finished, Robert sat with his eyes fixated on his empty glass completely speechless. Because of his silence, Michael questioned his decision to open up.

Robert wanted to say something to help. However, he was somewhat indecisive, because Michael was a spiritual man and he didn't know bible scriptures to reference. He didn't have any thought-provoking biblical commentary. All he had to offer was his story. Little did Robert know that was all he needed to help his new friend.

"Michael, look, man, I don't really know what to say. My heart goes out to you. But I do know from experience that if you react too soon, you may make the wrong decision." Michael nodded in agreement. However, he didn't feel inspired by Robert's public service announcement. Noticing Michael's nonchalant response, he went right into his testimony.

"Listen, my life in Chicago was great until things spiraled out of control. Early on, my marriage was good. To the naked eye, my wife and I were doing well. Things were going great with my career and she had a good-paying job working for an investment firm. In high school, I had a problem with drinking and my wife dabbled with smoking a joint from time to time. It was something we saw as normal. I remember the night we met, we both were high. I saw her at a party and approached her while she was smoking weed with mutual friends and we instantly hit it off. We eventually started dating and accepted each other's recreational habit, if you know what I mean. But, I hit a wall with my drinking right before our child was born. I've been an electrician for over seventeen years. While I was an apprentice, I went to the job site drunk and caused an electrical fire that almost destroyed the entire building. Luckily, my mentor covered for me. Almost losing my job with a baby on the way was enough to dial back the drinking. I felt we both had to change some things we were doing and begged her to slow down as well. But she wasn't trying to hear it."

Michael seemed confused about the timeline. "Wait, didn't you say you had a little one on the way? So she was smoking weed while she was pregnant?"

Robert nodded and continued, "Yep, the whole pregnancy. We argued constantly. I thank God my child didn't have any effects from it. Over time, her habit got worse. She went from weed to the powder. Once the coke came in to play, it was a lost cause.

She became a high-functioning addict. You would have never known she was a cokehead. However, that all changed a couple of years later when she got laid off and the money for her habit wasn't there. Like a true addict, she adapted and settled for crack. At that point, I had enough. She would go missing for days at a time. The day I left with my son, she was busted in a raid. She spent eight months in jail. Behind bars, she promised she would change and get her life together. Once she got out, she went right back to the drugs. I loved my wife, man. I had to make a tough decision and ended up filing for divorce because I didn't believe in her anymore. She cried and cried! Begged like crazy! I remember seeing this look in her eyes that seemed to say she's had enough. I almost stayed. Now, I wish I did."

Michael readjusted in his seat, wondering what he meant by wishing he stayed.

Robert continued, "I made a big mistake placing my trust in her to change. Like I said before, I loved her. I wanted to believe she would get better, but I just didn't believe in her. I realize now, my job was to trust and believe God concerning my wife. You may not believe this, but now, she is completely different. She remarried and has two kids. She's not only been drug free but volunteers as a drug counselor at her church. Her former boss changed companies and hired her. She's now their head analyst and doing well financially. I don't know if she would have turned out this way had I stayed. I was a provider, not a godly man. That's what she has now, and to be honest, that's probably what she always needed in her corner. Michael, I shared that story with you for a couple of reasons. First, don't let your anger or pain affect your decisions. You know better than I do. You know to trust God. Secondly, if your wife is crying out to you and in your heart of hearts you feel she is better than what she has done, believe God can change her. Man, don't throw away your marriage over this. To be honest, I wish cheating was my ex-wife's problem. I think it would have been easier to overcome. It's hell waiting to see if a person will ever leave drugs alone. I believe Jasmine loves you and will make the turnaround. I'm just saying, man, people like me can learn from you. You are exactly what your wife needs right now, a praying husband that has the ability to trust God while life is upside down. After all that I've said, the question is will you focus on Jasmine and what she's done or will you keep your eyes on God, realizing what he has done, is doing, and promised to do for you and your family?"

Tears rolled from Michael's eyes. Robert's testimony challenged him. Robert stood up and went to the restroom to give his mentor a minute to think. Michael tried his best to hide the conflict within. He struggled to find the confidence to lift his head. An elderly gentleman that sat across from them walked over and asked Michael if he was OK. Michael tried to regain his composure and answered, "Yes, sir. I'm all right."

The old man placed his hand on Michael's shoulder and spoke, "My name is Earl Henry, and

I've been around for eighty-one years, son. I know a hurting man when I see one. I don't know what you are going through, but I do know this. Watch what seed you put in the ground. If you plant doubt, despair, and defeat, Satan will use your tears to water those seeds and the only thing you will harvest is pain. Whatever you are going through, fight! Fight! There is a blessing after the battle."

Michael looked up with watery eyes and thanked Mr. Henry as he walked away with his grandson.

Before going their separate ways, Michael thanked Robert for the words of encouragement. "Big Rob, I appreciate you, man. I needed this. I gotta admit it's easier to store unchallenged faith and extremely tough to use it in turbulent times. But I promise you this, I will find a way to bounce back."

While Michael was being encouraged, Jasmine was slowly downgrading. Once again, Paige called to check on her and to ask a question. "Jas, how are you holding up?"

With a faint voice, Jasmine replied, "I'm numb all over, but I guess I'm still alive."

"Well, I hope my question gets your blood flowing again. Can I have Adrian's number please?

As Paige predicted, Jasmine voice grew stronger, "What? For what?"

Paige confidently answered, "I need to let him know what's going on. He needs to know your marriage is in critical condition because of his relationship with you. I also want to tell him contacting you will not be a good idea. I want to be the one to deliver the message because he doesn't need to hear from you at all."

Jasmine disagreed. "Paige, you don't understand. I think I should lay low and not say anything right now. The last thing I can afford is upset Adrian and cause him to pull the deal from Michael and his boss. I've done enough to my husband. The least I can do is stay away and not interfere with what he is trying to accomplish. Plus, I've already blocked Adrian's number. I know your intentions are good and I love you for being a sister to me. But you weren't there to see how calculated Michael's reactions were. It was scary. If I cause any more damage to him, I will be better off dead. Trust me on this one."

Paige understood and decided to cool her jets. "All right, I'll sit myself down somewhere. I guess I got riled up thinking about everything."

Paige and Robert's efforts provided a sense of normalcy to an otherwise tumultuous situation. Their agendas were the same, let the Fletchers talk. They felt the more they talked about it, the higher the possibility of the problem losing its potency. It was a great scientific approach; however, life's circumstances rarely adheres to science. Jasmine's confidence lasted as long as she talked to Paige. Equally, Michael found it difficult to stay spiritually motivated from Robert's testimony. The Fletcher's pain and regret in comparison to healing and restoration was as volatile as the stock market. Things were uncertain to say the least. Sooner or later, a decision had to be made. Jasmine's mind was made up. She desperately wanted her husband back. Giving up Adrian and all he presented was a welcomed task as opposed to losing her marriage. Unfortunately, all the cards were in her husband's hands. Internally, Michael resembled a war zone. Extrinsic motivation was short-lived. Intrinsic motivation didn't stand a chance. All the days encouraging others. All the efforts to live right. All his spiritual convictions. All the stored faith, they all seemed to be a no show at the most crucial moment of his life. He really needed God to just take care of it. He simply wanted it fixed. It was apparent he was electing to sit in the back seat and let Jesus grab the wheel. It was fair to assume Michael expected God to do him a solid because of the prior spiritual services he rendered to promote the kingdom. On the contrary, God was showing Michael his walk never secured a challenge-free life. Perhaps, promoting the kingdom required a well-placed storm not only to show others the power of God but to reveal to him the strength and weaknesses in his spiritual armor. Maybe Michael had to be confronted with a potential deal breaker that could separate him from his convictions. Two days passed without conversation between man and wife. He had begun to miss Jasmine; however, he refused to let her know it. Tracy called to check on their status and to inform him she was heading back to Los Angeles. She expressed her concern for them and like Robert and Mr. Henry, she also left Michael with a small nugget to consider.

"Listen, my good friend. I was thinking about everything and I wish I could say something to turn this all around for you. However, there's nothing any-one can say. It may simply come down to just remem-bering what God allowed to happen to his own."

Michael listened to see where Tracy was going.

"I guess what I'm trying to say is, if He would allow his son to be persecuted and crucified for the greater good, maybe just maybe your situation will turn out to be a benefit to others. If so, it all relies on how you handle this." Michael listened as Tracy ministered to him. Before they ended their phone conversation, she left him with a difficult request. "Promise me you will fight for her. She needs to see your strength." Michael felt Tracy was losing her mind. She basically asked him to set aside the pain his wife caused to show her how to deal with extreme adversity. He thought to himself, "Who does she think I am, Superman?"

Here was another person placing responsibil-ity on his shoulders. It was a clear indication that he couldn't sit back and expect God to restore order without any effort from him. Michael didn't want to embrace the role of being the sacrificial lamb. Yet the more he thought about it, even Jesus had a brief moment of wanting to pass the cup in the Garden of Gethsemane. Like his Savior, it will take getting out of his feelings and trusting God. He pictured life without Jasmine and the mere thought was incon-ceivable. However, every thought of keeping her was challenged with visions of her infidelity. As he drove down the interstate, everything seemed to overload his mind. The promotion, the incident, the words of encouragement, another man sleeping with his wife, finally he lost it. It could have appeared less dramatic had Michael tinted his windows. Passing drivers saw a man flailing his hands, as he seemed to be shouting in the empty cabin. He'd had enough! He desperately needed the Father and son talk. "Lord, I need to hear from you! No more representatives! I get it! I know you want me to stand for my marriage. I just don't know how! I'm hurting, man! How do you expect me to do this?" Suddenly, it was as if a passenger teleported into the seat. A small calm voice filled the cabin. "How do I expect you to do this? I expect you to live the words you encouraged others to live by. Michael, I appreciate the man you have become. But you were naive to think I wouldn't allow you to be tested. For any believer, the question isn't can you recite, teach, or preach my word, but can you live my word? Can you live it when you are leveled to the floor? Can you ignore what you feel and cling to what you believe? Will you ignore what this looks like and trust my voice? There are two things I see that have the potential to destroy you. It's your sight and your inability to forgive." Michael listened attentively as God continued. "Your belief is taking a hit because you are struggling with forgiveness. I want you to think back when you heard the sermon about Peter stepping out of the boat. As he walked on water, he began to forfeit his supernatural experience when he took his eyes off my Son. He used his eyes for the wrong purpose. He used them to focus on the conditions around him. Son, if you are having problems with your eyes, I suggest you handle this situation like a blind man. Deactivate your sight and trust what you hear, as my word speaks to you. I challenge you to see with your ears. Secondly, Peter subconsciously put a limit on how many times he was willing to forgive. My Son had to remind him that true forgiveness has no limitations. In regards to your wife, has she fallen so far from your grace to where it's impossible for her to receive mercy? Michael, once you address your conflict within, I am confident you will regain your footing. Now, are you still confused on exactly how I expect you to do this, as you say?" Michael got what he asked for, a meeting with THE MAN! Only thing, it wasn't the two-way conversation he anticipated. God allowed him time to reply and plead his case, but there was nothing to say after God spoke. At that point, Michael's blood pressure and anxiety leveled. He managed to laugh as he replied, "You always do that. When you speak, you take away our chance to vent. You make folks feel silly." Michael finally got the ultimate confirmation. It was time he lived his words.

Chapter 18

. . . Unfinished Business

Michael knew what he wanted. He loved his wife and nothing would matter without her. He regained some inner strength and planned to reconcile. However, before he could do so with a clear conscious, there was some unfinished business. He was a spiritual man, but he was a man. The reset button will be hit after his face to face with Adrian. Before putting things in motion, he contacted Ms. Sprewell the next day to get her perspective as a friend and as a boss.

"Tracy, how are you?"

She replied, "I'm doing great. What's going on with you? You sound better?"

Michael replied. "I'm getting there. I called to get your thoughts on something."

Tracy opened the door to her office, placed her purse and lunch on her desk, and grabbed her phone that was wedged between her head and shoulder.

"Woo, excuse me. I was walking into my office and my hands were full. Now, go ahead and shoot."

Michael began, "Well, I've decided to keep my marriage. I want to give my wife a chance to right her wrong. There's just one thing though. I have to confront Adrian Moore. I don't know if that will get me fired, destroy the real estate deal or what. I need the business advice and a little personal advice if you can separate the two." He braced himself expecting Tracy to respond like a boardroom executive.

On the contrary, she stayed in the friend zone. "Well, on the business side, the deal is done. There isn't anything he can do. Contracts are signed. To be honest, I wouldn't have stopped you either way. I wouldn't dare tell you not to fight for your wife. I wish my man would let somebody talk him out of fighting for me. I don't care who it is. We would have some problems."

Michael laughed, "Calm down. That man is probably fighting for you as we speak. Just don't put him in the position Jasmine has me in. Fighting for you then becomes an option."

She assured Michael, "Trust me, I won't put him through that. But seriously, my good friend, there's two things I want you to remember if you choose to confront him. Don't do anything that will get you locked up or killed and remember she allowed him to be the other man. I know you don't want to hear this and I hope it doesn't cause you to relapse, but she made him think it was OK to disrespect you and your marriage. If you must do this, pray first. If there is a chance you go to jail or a funeral home, I suggest you don't do it."

Although Michael didn't have a script or plan, he did know there weren't any premeditated intentions of violence. He simply wanted to put Adrian on high alert that any further contact with his wife would be the worst mistake of his life. He understood the dangers of such a meeting, but it had to take place. "I know what you are saying. I don't plan on acting a fool. Like you say, he was an opportunist. Jasmine gave him access. That's the toughest thing to accept, but it is what it is. I just hope he doesn't get cocky and say the wrong thing."

Tracy shouted, "And that's what I'm afraid of! What if he thinks he had a chance to take Jasmine from you? He will provoke you. Michael please be careful."

He promised Tracy he would do his absolute best to stay under control. "I'm actually expecting some arrogance, but it will be OK." Michael felt better knowing things wouldn't affect his job. Next step was to arrange a meeting. He remembered Adrian gave out his business cards the day at the building. He pulled it out of his wallet and made the call. He was prepared to hear Adrian's voice. Instead, a lady answered. Michael gave his first name only and told her who he worked for and requested a meeting. She placed him on hold and returned seconds later, "Thanks for holding. Mr. Moore can meet with you tomorrow at noon. If that's OK, I can email or text you the address of the meeting."

Michael agreed to the arrangement and pre-pared to reintroduce himself to Jasmine's secret lover. He thought about calling her and have her join the powwow. He ultimately decided against it fearing the sight of them together could cause him to go into a rage, especially when he miraculously held it together the first time. As he sat in his hotel room, perhaps for the last evening, he went through several scripts. "I'm going to start off saying…If he says this…Then I'll hit him with…and then…" Before he started argu-ing with the imaginary Adrian, he looked in the mir-ror and realized he sounded a tad bit psychotic. "No script, just say what needs to be said."

After a decent night of sleep, a complimentary wake-up call came from the front desk. Michael got up with a noticeable assertiveness. He packed the few items he had and checked out of the hotel. Once he arrived at the address he was given, he parked his car and took a few minutes to gather himself. He walked into the office building, gave his name, and waited for Adrian. Totally oblivious, Adrian came out to greet Michael with a smile on his face.

"Michael, how are you? What can I do for you?"

Without smiling, Michael requested they go somewhere they could talk privately. Once they were alone, he opened up. "I'm not here to waste time, so I'm going to try and make myself as clear as possible. First, you need to know who I am. My last name is Fletcher. Does that ring a bell?"

Adrian's smile straightened. He quickly realized why Michael was there. He needed a moment to strategize. Michael's revelation quickly had him on the ropes. In efforts to regain his footing, he utilized the proverbial standing eight count boxers get when they've been rocked with a right hook. He did so by deflecting. "Hold on. Wait a minute! I'm not sure I follow. Why would that ring a bell?"

Understanding the awkward position he put Adrian in, he anticipated a dumbfounded response. Michael became intimidating as he gritted his teeth and replied, "Look, let's stop the games! Trying to play dumb won't work. You know exactly who I am. You also know sleeping with my wife has brought me face-to-face with you. You have no idea how close you came to death when you introduced her as your girlfriend!"

Michael's plan to stay under control quickly detoured. If he wasn't careful, his next stop was going to be jail, the hospital, or the funeral home. He had to find a way to keep from overheating. He attempted to refocus with his next statement. "But as hard as it is to admit, my wife is to blame for most of this. She gave you something she no longer hold the rights too. She made you feel it was OK to sleep with her, disrespect me, and disrespect our marriage. I have to man up and call it like it is. At the end of the day, she gave you the opportunity. It was free and you took it. But by her being married, I would assume a smart business man like yourself would have known it was going to cost you eventually."

After finding his equilibrium, Adrian fired back. "Look, it's unfortunate things turned out this way, but it's not costing me anything! I mean, like you say, she knew the risks better than me. It was her job to respect you and your marriage. Not mine."

Michael took offense to Adrian's arrogant counterpunch. It was clear he wasn't going to be overly apologetic. Tension began to rise at a noticeable pace as they went back and forth. Michael replied, "I didn't come here to plead with you! I came to tell you straight up, man to man, if you come near my wife again, it would be the worst mistake of your life."

Deep down, Adrian knew he was wrong for his part in the affair. He knew being involved with a married woman was dangerous; however, his feelings for Jasmine proved to be stronger than anyone would have imagined. He heard Michael's threat, but he mentally swatted it away like a nagging fly. He had fallen in love with her, and somewhere in his mind, Jasmine being married wasn't big enough to be a deterrent. He felt they were getting closer. Adrian actually believed the odds of her choosing him over her husband had improved to a fifty-fifty chance. His next statement challenged Michael's resolve.

"Jasmine will have to tell me she doesn't want me, not you! It's her decision, not yours!" Adrian was literally fighting for a woman he illegally attained.

Once again, Michael appeared to lose his cool. He toppled a chair and took aggressive steps toward Adrian. Adrian stepped back and stood in a defensive stance.

Meanwhile, Jasmine hadn't talked to her husband and she desperately needed to hear his voice.

Since the incident, she'd called him thousands of times. She was tired of sitting in the house and she didn't have the exuberance to go anywhere. Therefore, she settled for sitting in her car inside the garage. Every love song that played over the radio caused her to cry. It was as if she was in high school crying because her boyfriend took another girl to the prom. She decided to call Michael again. This time, she got what she wanted. He finally answered; however, Jasmine's timing was terrible. Instantly, she found herself in the middle of a standoff.

Although immersed in a duel of wills, Michael heard his phone ring and instinctively looked at the screen. At first glance, he wasn't going to answer Jasmine's call. His focus was on getting Adrian to comply.

Perhaps, Jasmine's phone call was a modern-day version of the ram in the bush. There was only one slight difference. In comparison to Abraham preparing to sacrifice Isaac on Mt. Moriah, Michael's intentions wouldn't qualify as a sacrificial kill. Time froze as he contemplated allowing Jasmine to tell Adrian it was over. It wasn't necessarily the male dominant thing to do, but it could end the battle and prevent their confrontation from taking a nasty turn. In his carnal mind, he wanted to physically destroy Mr. Moore. Even Peter, the same man God referenced, the disciple who stepped out of the boat to walk on water, was the same guy who sliced off a soldier's ear to protect Jesus. Although Michael wasn't protecting Jesus, he was protecting his wife; and to his defense, the Bible does say love your wife like God loves the church. He wondered if taking care of Adrian could actually be allowed due to a biblical precedent. Fearing God wouldn't see the rationale in his spiritual interpretation, he realigned his thinking.

Then, he remembered God saying, "Trust what you hear." He became convinced hearing the phone ring was a sign. Therefore, he chose to answer, hoping that allowing Jasmine to speak would end this fiasco.

Jasmine knew things were tense the second she heard Michael's voice. He shouted, "Hello!"

Jasmine responded, "Michael, is everything OK?"

He answered, "No, everything is not OK! I'm standing here looking your boyfriend in the eyes. Obviously, he is convinced you love him and he refuses to let go until you tell him."

Jasmine listened with a blank stare. She had mixed emotions about their meeting. On one hand, she became hopeful realizing if Michael was there to confront Adrian, there was a strong chance he had decided to keep his marriage. On the contrary, her hands began to tremble as frightening thoughts filled her head. She hoped Adrian wasn't crazy enough to give detailed information of their encounters. If he decided to reveal any pillow talk, it would seal her fate. Jasmine knew there were times she said too much while in the heat of the moment. Adrian often asked if she wondered what life would be like if they were together. In those moments, she displayed characteristics of a cheating man. She said things to Adrian that sounded like realistic possibilities. Deep down, she didn't mean any of it.

Being thrust into the showdown, she had to face the music and pray Adrian didn't rattle off several misleading conversations.

Michael put the phone on speaker mode. "Jasmine, can you hear me? I have you on speaker!"

Jasmine knew she had to respond. She didn't want her husband to do anything drastic. Calmly, she answered, "Yes, Michael, I'm here."

Adrian shouted so she could hear him, "Jasmine, baby, please tell me what's going on. Please say it's me you want!"

Michael's battle within a battle continued as spirit and flesh remained in a slugfest. In the background, Michael's voice blended in while Adrian spoke, "My wife is not your damn baby! Boy, I'll kill you where you stand!" Michael's anger had overrun its banks. He moved closer to corner Adrian. Jasmine felt the rise in action. She knew this was her chance to show Michael she wanted her life back. Jasmine shouted through the phone. "No! No, I want my husband! I love my husband! We were a mistake, Adrian. We were a big mistake!"

Adrian's face fell. Michael stopped in his tracks and gave him an aggressive stare. It was a look that mimicked a victorious male lion after establishing dominance and rights to the pride. Michael roared, "There you go! Don't come near my wife again!"

Adrian was shell shocked as Jasmine screamed through the phone, "Michael, Michael, come home! Please!" Hearing Jasmine beg her husband to come to her infuriated him.

Adrian should have taken this lick on the chin like a champ. It was normal for him to watch women he dated fall to ruins after he called it quits. Obviously, this vantage point caused him to feel differently, mostly because he was the one being relieved of duty. The change of dynamics instantly caused him to become the scorned lover. Rejection caused him to try and wreck what he couldn't have. He redirected his attention to Michael. Ironically, he no longer wanted to hear Jasmine speak. She had made her choice. However, he did want her to listen to what he was about to say to her husband. With his hands up in submission, he conceded. Instead of extending congratulations, he attempted to inform Michael of some privileged information.

"OK, I guess that's it! You win, but I think you should know what you really have at home."

Jasmine held her breath hoping Adrian wouldn't expose her.

Michael cut him off, "I don't need you or any other man to tell me what I have at home! I think you are pissed off because you had no idea WHO she had at home!"

Adrian tried his best not to show any chink in his armor with Michael's confident statement. Although he remained prideful, he realized Michael Fletcher was a formidable opponent. It was more to this dude than Jasmine led him to believe. It became more apparent Jasmine used him. Anger filled him because he actually fell in love with her.

Michael continued, "She chose her husband over you and now you want to tell me about the pillow talk in the dark. I guess you want to tell me all the things that were said after having sex. How y'all wished and imagined being together. Or maybe you want to tell me about all the *what ifs* and *maybe one day* type of stuff that she brought up. Right?"

Adrian didn't respond, so Michael shouted louder, "Am I right? Is that what you want to tell me?"

Adrian stared at him, while Jasmine listened. She took a quick breath like a dolphin coming up for air, before holding it again to hear the rest of the conversation. Michael continued, "If that's what you want to say, don't bother. I know how the game goes! When the lights are off, you dream big, but you can wake up now! All it was ever going to be was a dream. I can look at your face and tell you are used to calling the shots. Funny thing is you forgot even the player can get played. You screwed up by thinking you had the game on lock and my wife was yours for the taking. What? You thought you were in control of Jasmine? Like I told you, I know what I have at home. You can't control her. Michael thought about what he said and added, "Hell! Obviously, I can't either!"

Jasmine felt extremely low. Through the phone Michael heard painful whispers, "I'm so sorry, Michael. I don't deserve you."

Adrian grew tired of the whole situation. Jasmine was gone and there was no need to try and fight for her.

"It's whatever man! I have nothing to say to you or her. Just get out!"

Michael gave his last warning, "If we have to meet again, it will be on your doorstep!"

Adrian issued a warning of his own. "If you come to my door, I will protect my house!"

Michael replied, "Just know if I come, you and your house will be destroyed!"

He slammed the door so hard, pictures fell off of the wall.

Michael ended the call as he walked out. Jasmine thought she was disconnected by mistake and tried to call back, but Michael didn't answer. She had no clue what his next move was going to be.

Although he drove off satisfied with his meeting with Mr. Moore, he knew he went off script without consent of his heavenly director. He was content, but God wasn't necessarily pleased with his decision to confront Adrian. Oddly, setting Adrian straight was the easy part. The biggest obstacle remained front and center in his heart. Forgiveness was a much bigger opponent than Adrian Moore. He still had to endure the gauntlet of pain, pride, and frustration and decide if his wife was worth keeping. If he chose to stay, he had to do so without beating her over the head with her transgressions. For many people, that is no easy task and Michael wasn't sure he was any different from the rest. While thinking, he realized he hadn't talked to Paige. He couldn't imagine her being OK with Jasmine's actions. He wanted to hear her thoughts, so he gave her a call.

"Paige, what's going on, girl? I haven't heard from you in a while."

She was somewhat surprised, "Hey! How are you?"

Michael replied, "Um, let's just say I'm going to be OK eventually. I know you are aware of what had happened to us."

Paige slowly answered, "Yes, I am aware and I hate it. What Jasmine did was selfish and flat out stupid. However, when I look into her eyes, I can tell she's broken by her actions. Honestly, I believe she's broken enough to never go down that road again. I also know losing you will destroy her. Big brother, I haven't reached out to you because I felt you needed time to process all of this."

Michael returned, "Yeah, *process*. Problem is you have to be able to think clearly in order to process. This is hard, Paige. I mean, I don't know how to describe the battle within me."

Paige attempted to encourage him. "Michael your marriage is still worth it. Don't give up on her. You are the head of your family. Whether you agree or not, as your wife's leader, it's your job to usher her back to God. Pray for her Michael."

Hearing Paige say that reminded him of Robert's advice.

She carried on, "I know you understand when I say forgiving people is a fight sometimes. There will be days when things are going great, and just seeing her smile and play like she used to will make you angry. Satan will play with your head and say she's tricking you, so you can let your guard down. You will have to fight those thoughts by trusting in God. Trusting the Lord is key. Remember when Peter couldn't catch a fish no matter how hard he tried? Jesus showed up and told him to cast his net again. All he had to do was trust and obey Him. You know how that story ended. The boy caught so many fish it was ridiculous. Big brother fight off your feelings and cling to your source. I'm simply saying, love and trust your wife, but trust God more. He may allow our lives to become unbalanced at times, but he will never let us fall. So, boy, go back to your wife and enjoy your next level of life. And speaking of that, from what I heard from Robert, you are in a position to bless your girl with a new Jaguar for her birthday. Hint. Hint."

Michael smirked, "Oh, she won't be getting that this year!"

Paige shouted, "Boy, I'm talking about me! As hard as I'm working counseling the two of you, I deserve it."

Michael laughed, "You may be right, sis! We'll see what God puts on my heart."

Paige answered, "I just told you what he's going to put on your heart. Don't be hardheaded! Just make sure you move when he says get up and go to the dealership and get my Jag!"

After hanging up, Michael couldn't help but notice the consistent references to Peter. Clearly, God was pounding his assignment into his spirit. "Trust me! Trust me! Trust me! Forgive! Forgive! Forgive!" The more he meditated on that message, optimism for reconciliation began to build! He decided to pull into an empty parking lot and take time to consider everything that has happened and everything that was told to him. He sat totally engulfed in prayer. Crying throughout, he'd reached a final decision.

The time for restoration had come. Instead of calling or texting Jasmine, Michael simply drove home. He had no idea what he was going to say when he saw his wife, but deep down, he couldn't wait to get there. His love for her became the dominant emotion. He just wanted to feel normal again. Free to love her without reservation. It was a choice he made and he was going in full throttle. The anger and pain disappeared. Her adultery was no longer the biggest item on the menu. He internally gave way to the fact that Jasmine was the biggest part of him.

Jasmine sat nervously on the couch, once again scrolling through her photo gallery with watery eyes. She heard the front door open. She initially thought it was one of the kids. She wiped her tears to disguise her mood and turned around. Mrs. Fletcher literally became frozen in place, as she saw her husband standing in the foyer. Her mouth was open in shock while single tears gracefully cascaded down her cheeks. One by one, each teardrop had a message for Michael. He attentively listened as they explained the pain in her heart. Silence had never been so roman-tic. They looked beyond each other's outer appear-ance and connected spiritually. What they had went beyond flesh. It was evident; they were truly the match made in heaven. Jasmine was overtaken by emotion. Her cheeks began to tremble, and her hands were shaking. Her eyes were weak and whimpered for attention. She wasn't sure what she was allowed to do. She desperately wanted to run into Michael's arms and recreate the scene from the airport in Los Angeles. Wanting his touch was an understatement. She needed his touch! To be wrapped in his arms, comfortably tucked away in his cocoon of love, pas-sion, and safety would undoubtedly reset her life.

Being a talented astute gentleman, Michael picked up her frequency and simply stretched out his long basketball arms to usher her into his heart. While she seemed to run to him in slow motion, Michael had the opportunity to examine his forever, as she approached. Her eagerness to reach him spoke to his spirit. Jasmine was his air, and without her, there was no way he could breathe. Any scenario that didn't include her in his life was a death sentence. His eyes began to mirror Jasmine's eyes. Tears poured out like heavenly rain. Michael stood like a true warrior, a real man! He was going to fight for them and losing was not an option! Jasmine's man wanted the world to know he was in love with his wife!

Once she reached her destination, her eyes relaxed and closed in relief. All she wanted was the opportunity to right her wrong. Michael did not disappoint her. Like all the times before, he gave that gift from his heart.

The decor of the foyer and living room was common, yet the moment was majestic!

About the Author

Lawrence Etienne is a dedicated educator in the Houston area with over twenty years of experience. He is a proud graduate of Texas Southern University where he received a Bachelor's Degree in Telecommunications. Over the years, Lawrence has inspired his students to express themselves through various forms of writing. He feels the ability to capture the sentiments of others ultimately creates a connection between the reader and author. He truly loves people and values relationships; therefore, writing is a way for him to communicate with each reader and cultivate relationships. His creativeness allows him to be entertaining while also being impactful. On a personal note, Lawrence is a proud father and loving husband. He considers his family his greatest inspiration. Above all else, he values his relationship with his Heavenly Father. He is committed to writing novels that will entertain, yet provoke thought concerning the things of God.

CPSIA information can be obtained
at www.ICGtesting.com
Printed in the USA
FFHW011901041218
49749623-54207FF